Will Hunter's Last Gamble

When Will Hunter, the well-known wagon-master, settled down with a widow-woman who'd caught his eye, his friends knew it wouldn't last. And, sure enough, one month after the last wagon train left Abilene for Sacramento, a party of settlers tempted Will with big bonuses to lead them to California.

The winter snows in the high hills make it dangerous to travel and although Will agrees to undertake the commission it is against his better judgement.

As death stalks the trail, the intrepid ex-waggoner takes the biggest gamble of his life as he fights against all the odds.

By the same author

The Land Grabbers
The Man From Socorro
Warbuck
Oliver's Kingdom
Where the Condor Flies
Missouri Man
Rodeo Round-Up

Will Hunter's Last Gamble

Curt Longbow

ROBERT HALE · LONDON

First published in Great Britain 2004

ISBN 0 7090 7612 6

Robert Hale Limited
Clerkenwell House
Clerkenwell Green
London EC1R 0HT

Typeset by
Derek Doyle & Associates, Liverpool.
Printed and bound in Great Britain by
Antony Rowe Limited, Wiltshire

ONE

Eddie Doolan sat idly shuffling the cards. He was thinking about Will Hunter and his crazy idea about retiring after his next caravan trail to California. The idea was ridiculous! The guy was only in his mid-forties, for God's sake! He also wondered about the widow-woman Will had mentioned. Lucky bastard! But he couldn't see Will settling down to a humdrum married life on a ranch after years of adventuring, free to come and go when he liked and with an eye for the women.

He concluded he would have to have a private word with him. Now, he waited for Will and the other two card-players to come back from the pisshouse. His well-cared-for hands moved lovingly over the cards as he waited.

He had a tidy stash of dollars and coins, which a man standing close by at the bar was interested in. Billy, known as the Goat, because of his smell, was on the run from the state pen and he was waiting patiently for the card-school to break up. He wanted that stash badly. Whoever walked away with the pot was in for a bushwhacking. He waited patiently.

The three men came back and settled themselves at the table. Doc McLochry, disgruntled that Lady Luck had forsaken him, looked sourly at the others.

'Well, let's get on with it, fellers!'

Zac, the peddler of pots and pans when he wasn't being hired by Will Hunter as one of his drivers, only grinned. He'd lost least of all. He wasn't above doing a little cheating if things got tough. Will, he knew, never showed any resentment when he was taken to the cleaners. He took his losses lightly. But then, Will was a well-respected wagon-train boss and always in demand during the season. He could afford to lose a little.

Now, of course, the season for taking the caravan trail to California was over. The last wagon train had set off a month earlier, to arrive in California before the snows came. Will Hunter must now wait until spring before organizing another trip.

Doc McLochry belched as he waited for the cards to be dealt. His hands were unsteady. He needed another shot of rotgut to steady them. He too had been thinking of Will and his plans.

He laughed inwardly. Plans went wrong. Look how his own plans had gone wrong. He'd come to America, a newly qualified young doctor, eager to cure the new world's ills, and look at him now, twenty-five years later, a drunken bum who had to have a couple of stiff drinks before he could dig a bullet out of a man's body. He'd not set the world on fire and no one would grieve for him if he dropped dead in this sleazy saloon.

Zac thought Will's plans for his future were just wishful thinking and that Will was drunker than usual or he wouldn't have held forth as he had done. His mention of a widow-woman was another of his dreams. A widow-woman indeed! He couldn't think of any widow-woman willing to take him on. Will had never been known to stick to one woman longer than it took to pass through a town or settlement and all the women he usually met were whores in saloons. He couldn't see Will settling down. No sir!

Eddie was dealing cards when the batwing doors crashed open and the man walked in. Every eye in the saloon turned to the newcomer who stood and surveyed the smoke-filled room. He was short, with a long grey beard, and tufty grey hair showing beneath a greasy Stetson. His clothes and boots were dust-laden. He looked as if he was a saddle tramp, except for the expensive well-oiled twin Colts strapped low down on his hips. All recognized a man who meant business.

'I'm looking for a man called Will Hunter,' the little man bellowed in a deep baritone voice that didn't match his stature. Will sat back in his chair, pushing his Stetson further back from his forehead.

'Who wants to know?' he asked quietly.

Billy the Goat, standing close by at the bar, turned a little so that his right hand was free. It hovered over his low-slung gun. At the same time he pulled his hat well over his eyes with the other hand. He was always on his guard against strangers.

The newcomer studied Will Hunter and the three men with him.

'Any of you know Will Hunter?'

'I'm Hunter. What's your business?' Will leaned forward, one hand on the card-table and the other down at his side, a fraction away from his gun.

The old man took off his hat and scratched his bald pate.

'Thank God! I've looked all over town for you! I'm Jack Broadbent and me and some others want you to lead us over to California. We heard you were in town.'

Will relaxed.

'California? My next trek will be in the spring. You come back then and we'll talk.'

'No, we want to go right now! It's urgent for us all. We're willing to put up two thousand dollars each over and above the going rate for you and your men. Are you on?'

Will laughed.

'You've sure come at a bad time, mister. The last wagon trains left here a month ago. It's too late to start off now. If the snows come early we could be marooned in the hills. You'd be crazy even to think of going now. It takes at least three months on a good trek. In bad times it could take twice that time, especially if we hit Indian trouble. There's still a bunch out there who make war on us freighters, and not only Indians. We come up against desperadoes hoping to make a fast buck from what we're freighting. It's no good, mister. None of the wagon masters would consider the idea. You'll have to wait until spring.'

'We can't wait, Mr Hunter. I'm a storekeeper among other things and I told my partner I'd be out there with a load of supplies before spring. And there's six families wanting to travel. Think of it, Mr Hunter, you'd be picking up twelve thousand dollars above your usual rate. What d'you say?'

Will rubbed his chin. The proposition was tempting. He looked at the other three men. All had been with him on other trips. They knew the conditions as he did himself and all looked interested. His dream of marrying his widow-woman and buying himself a good spread could be closer than he'd expected.

'I've got to think about it, mister. It's a risk and a gamble and it's crazy. On the other hand . . .' His eyes swept over the other three men. If they came with him, they would get good bonuses too. He made a decision.

'Look, Mr Broadbent, you come back here tonight at sundown and bring your friends with you and we'll thrash the matter out. I've got a right to meet the men I'll be travelling with. OK?'

'Fine!' Will watched the man move over to the bar and down a couple of stiff drinks before leaving the saloon. Will turned to the others.

'He's crazy! No man in his right mind would tackle that trail at this time of year! We'll spell it out to them when they turn up tonight.'

Eddie Doolan grinned.

'But that extra cash sounds mighty good, Will. You said you wanted a last stash before you put your plans in action!' He was joking and wanted to needle Will. He was astonished at Will's reaction.

'Yeah, well, it's mighty tempting. If I thought there was a chance of making a swift run of it, I'd take him on! No doubt about it!'

'A pity they hadn't moseyed in a little sooner,' mused Eddie. 'I could have done with some extra cash.'

'Me too,' Zac put in eagerly. 'I've got an eye on some new-fangled washboards that I think the women will love but they cost money, and I was asked several times on my rounds whether I had any of the new charcoal-burning irons. What in hell a woman wants an iron for beats me!' he grumbled and took another drink.

The four resumed their card-playing and a patient Billy the Goat watched as the stash of cash grew higher and the fortunes of the players varied. But he was a patient man and he grinned inwardly as he thought of the moment when he cold-cocked the lucky winner. That cash would see him on his way in style for a few weeks to come.

Every now and again when a new round of drinks was brought, one of the group would start off speculating again about the old man's proposition. The thought of that extra cash nagged at them all.

The doc, now more than a little drunk, belched and patted his middle.

'I could do with a steak and hash browns. What about eating, fellers? We can eat and make out a case why we don't take on those fellers and why we should pass on the best proposition you've had all season, Will.'

Will hiccuped.

'I haven't passed up on it yet, Doc. I been thinking about it. Maybe we could strike lucky.'

Eddie nearly dropped the cards he was gathering up.

'You don't really mean that? We all know the conditions. The trail is tough enough in good times, but tackling that trail in winter would be hell! What if the snow came before we got over the mountains?'

Will shrugged.

'I been thinking of that too. There's a way station just beyond Long Drop Pass. It would be closed down for the winter but at a pinch we could hole up there if need be.'

'You're mad!' Doc McLochry said sharply. 'It sounds as if you're already considering it!'

'Just thinking of the possibilities, is all,' Will answered airily, the extra booze making the proposition more attractive. 'An offer like that doesn't come every day! Think of it! Bonuses for all of us, and a new start for me sooner than I expected!'

'And sooner than your widow-woman expected!' Zac said slyly. 'Maybe she wouldn't be ready to face the preacher!'

They all laughed but Will scowled at him.

'You don't believe me about the widow-woman, do you? If you think I'm going to tell you who she is, then you're going to be disappointed! I don't want anyone else going after her when they know she's available!'

'Huh!' Eddie Doolan spat on the earth floor

and ground the glob into the ground with the toe of his boot. 'It's like that, is it? Are you sure your widow-woman isn't one of the girls in Charlie's Place? You know, the one called Rosie? You were always sniffing round her!'

Will half-rose from his chair and leaned over the table. He clawed Eddie by the throat and dragged him forward.

'Why, you dirty-mouthed scumbag! What are you saying? You think I'm a liar? Everybody knows Rosie! She's anybody's any time! Do you think I'd *marry* her?' He shook Eddie viciously and dropped him back in his chair.

'Steady on, Will,' Doc McLochry protested. 'Don't start a brawl. We all know that you and Rosie were more than good friends!'

'Don't you start!' snarled Will. 'I'm just as friendly with Rosie as you are . . . all of you! So you can all reckon I wouldn't be thinking of getting hogtied to her! The widow-woman I've in mind has a boy of ten and she's young enough to give me a son of my own! Now I'm saying no more than that. Now, what about another drink and we'll forget all this bullshit. We'll have to settle this about whether we take a gamble and set off for California. Who's willing to take a gamble?'

The men looked at each other. It was Eddie's hand that went up first.

'I'm a gambler so I'll give it my best shot.' He

looked at the others. 'I'm no yellow-belly!'

Zac and the doc looked at each other, the doc thinking: what the hell, my life isn't worth shit, and Zac thinking: I'm scared but I'm damned if I'll let those bastards know how I feel.

They both raised their hands.

Then a cough made them all look up at the man standing close by. He grinned at them.

'I've been listening to what you fellers been saying. I'm Billy and I sure want to go to California. If you want an extra hand I'm your man!'

Will looked hard at the stranger. He smelled bad. Will reckoned he should be dunked into the nearest horse-trough. The fellow was slight but sinewy. His face, from what he could see under the man's greasy Stetson, was young but marred by a scar near his mouth which showed red under a sparse growth of whisker. His checked shirt was dusty and torn and his pants and boots well-worn and muddied. This feller had been on the road for some time.

'You come far, mister?' Will asked.

The man laughed showing badly stained yellow teeth.

'You might say that. I need to get to California fast. My old man is dying,' he said quickly, knowing he had to have a reason for travelling in winter.

'Sorry to hear that, son. You reckon he'll be

still with us by the time we get there . . . that is, if we go?'

Billy gave a long-drawn-out sigh and rubbed his eyes with the back of a dirty hand.

'He's in God's hands, mister. Let's hope he waits until I get to see him one last time. We was always close, was my pa and me.' Billy thought of his long-dead father who'd belted hell out of him every day until he'd run away when he was sixteen and never saw him again.

'I reckon I'll need extra drivers as I've freight of my own to ship to California. If we decide to go, you're on. Where are you staying? At Mrs Betts's rooming-house?'

'No. I reckon I'll be bedding down with my horse at the livery stable. I want to be out of this town tomorrow whether with you or without you.'

Will looked at him suspiciously.

'Sounds like you're in a mighty hurry!'

'Yeah. Like I said, I aim to get to Pa as soon as possible.'

Will didn't believe him. There was something twitchy about the feller, but it was none of his business. If they were to roll those wagons out of town he would be a useful man and one less recruit to round up.

So when the small group of men came into the bar at precisely six o'clock, the four men were just finishing their grub. Will wiped his greasy lips on his sleeve and nodded to the old man leading the group.

'Howdy!'

The old man nodded.

'These are my friends who want you to lead us to California.'

Will surveyed the bunch of tough-looking men who eyed him curiously.

Standing out from the rest was a preacher. He had a hawklike face and burning eyes. A regular hellfire merchant, Will reckoned. Beside him stood a tough-looking guy who might be a dirt farmer. There was also a long rangy feller with twin Colts, hugging a Spencer repeating rifle. A useful shooter if it came to a fight with hungry Indians.

There was also a tall, bony man who surprisingly had a Negro manacled to his wrist. Will took a deep breath when he saw the squat muscular black man.

'Must he be cuffed like that, mister? Do you reckon to keep him hogtied all the way to California?'

'Nope! I've got leg chains for when we're on the trail. He'll not run far in them!' The tall thin man laughed and it sounded like a bellow from a drum. 'I want to take him back alive, but if he tries to get away I'll shoot him in the leg. He knows that!'

Will took another look at the prisoner. He

didn't look dangerous, more hangdog, as if his life had been nothing but beatings. Will felt unaccountably sorry for him and an instant dislike of the thin man.

Then he turned to look at the last man to walk in.

'I'm Hank Holden,' the man said briefly before Will could say a word. He held out his hand for Will to shake. He sounded and looked more refined than the other men.

'Pleased to meet you. May I ask why you're in a hurry to get to California? You know the danger at this time of year?'

'Yes,' the man answered firmly, 'I do, but it's none of your business why I'm going! I'm paying like the rest of them and that's it!' He gave Will a hard stare as if to challenge him to take up the matter. Will was taken aback.

'Suit yourself, mister.' He turned to the rest of the men. 'Me and my men have discussed the situation and argued both for and against travelling now. You must all realize there is a great risk in setting off now. If the snows come early we could be in big trouble. Does that worry any of you?'

They all shook their heads. It was the old man Jack Broadbent who seemed to be their spokesman.

'We've talked it all out. We all have our reasons for getting to California and we want to take the gamble.'

'So be it! Can you all be ready to ride out pronto!'

'Yeah. We've all been packed up and ready to go for days! But there's something else you should know.'

'And what's that?' Will looked hard at them all.

Jack Broadbent grinned.

'No need to look worried, mister, but there's three lone females coming along too. Betsy Goddard and two young girls!' He winked at Will. 'They're not paying for the privilege of riding with us, but Betsy reckons they'll pay in other ways . . . if you get my meaning!'

Will kept a wooden face and nodded but inwardly he groaned. Three loose women with no men of their own! It could be a recipe for disaster if the men started fighting over them! He gulped. On second thoughts, the promise of the extra $12,000 was worth the risk!

He nodded.

'No problem,' he said easily. 'I hope they're good cooks!'

Everyone laughed. Who cared what kind of cooks they were!

TWO

The four men looked at each other when the ill-assorted bunch had gone. That was it. They were committed.

'I hope we did the right thing,' Zac said gravely, and rubbed his chin nervously.

Will saw growing doubt in the other men's eyes.

'Pull yourself together, Zac!' he said sharply. 'Of course we've done the right thing! We've got to make an early start and we've got to impress on those hicks that we've got to force-march from early morning until late at night! It's going to be gruelling but it can be done. We take extra horses and wagons for breakdowns and, if the worst comes to the worst, we can kill the extra horses for food – not that it will come to that,' he amended as he saw alarm in Zac's eyes. Will reckoned Zac was the one to watch. He was going to be the weakest link. He turned to Doc McLochry.

'Doc, you got your gear? I take it you'll carry all the medicines you have in your office?'

'Yeah, and my instruments are always ready in my black bag. I'm also taking my dentist's chair. It might come in useful!'

Will nodded.

'Then there'll be no more drinking tonight, fellers. We've got a lot of work to do before dawn. Zac, your freight wagon ready to roll?'

'Yeah. I've no other way to store my goods. I reckon I can be ready to leave as soon as you blow the whistle!'

'Good, and what about you, Eddie?'

Eddie laughed.

'I've got my cards and dice and a change of clothing in my warbag and I'm ready to ride at any time.'

'So you can drive one of my wagons along with this guy here.' Will pointed at Billy who was finishing off a mug of ale and had turned to watch proceedings. He grinned and nodded at Eddie.

'So we're going to be buddies, mister! Can you drive a wagon?'

Eddie bristled. 'Of course I can drive a wagon! I was brought up on a dirt farm before I broke loose and found an easier way of earning a living! And I can shoot too. How are you in the shooting stakes?'

Billy laughed a little recklessly.

'I'll show you, mister.' Before any of them guessed his intention he drew his gun fast and aimed for one of the hanging lamps swinging from a rafter. It exploded into shards of glass and everyone in the saloon ducked.

Then came the angry expostulation from the saloonkeeper, who ordered him out of his saloon but not before he handed over five dollars for the damage. Billy was going to brazen it out but saw several of the customers line up beside the owner; he backed off throwing five dollars at the man and then giving Eddie a sour look.

'I'll see you fellers outside,' he said gruffly.

Will took a deep breath.

'I'm sorry about the ruckus, Charlie,' he said quietly. 'I've just taken him on as a driver. He'll be out of town tomorrow.'

Charlie nodded.

'A good thing too. I was in half a mind to call in the sheriff. I reckon he's just some tumbleweed, going nowhere in particular.'

'He says he wants to get to California to see his old man again.' Charlie laughed.

'With that accent? He's no Californian even if he reckons he's got an old man there. I think he's just a no-good hick taking the advantage of you folk going to California.'

'So you heard what we were discussing?'

'Of course. I think everyone here heard you.

None of you was keeping your voices down. I will say this, Will, you've got a big heart in your belly to start off. Isn't it a bit late in the year to go gallivanting off?'

Will shrugged.

'Money talks, Charlie. Yeah, money talks. But we've got a lot to do before morning so we'll stop gabbing.' He turned to the others. 'What you all waiting for? Hadn't you all better go about your business? We'll line up the wagons in the usual place by dawn, and I'm going to seek out Tommy Two Feathers, sober him up and get him in some condition to ride with us. Now get!'

Charlie shook his head slowly as the four men left the saloon. He didn't think much of their chances. If they won through to Sacramento, the epic journey would become a legend. If not, those men would just disappear from history.

He went to draw more beer from a barrel for a cowboy waving an empty mug under his nose. He soon forgot Will as he coped with his rowdy customers.

The streets of Abilene were still teeming with townsfolk. Riders and wagons still rode the dirt streets. There was the smell of cows pervading the town as the cattle-sheds were full waiting for the next train going to the abbatoirs back East.

Will knew he would find Tommy Two Feathers

in that shack just out of town called Jontie's. There, in the murky smoky depths of a rough pine-built cabin would be a group of half-breeds and Indians, the outcasts of Abilene. This was their watering-hole. It smelled of damp earth, human sweat and stale beer. Will's nose wrinkled as he opened the batwing doors and stood just inside. He saw men sitting on boxes around upturned beer-barrels which served as tables. A tall muscular man with a beer-gut stood behind a plank which rested on two barrels. It was his makeshift bar.

The man was dark with hawklike Indian features but his eyes were blue, the only indication that he'd had a white man as a father. The blue eyes and the name Jontie were the only attributes his father had given him.

Now he stepped from behind his plank bar and came over to Will whom he recognized, Will having come on this mission many times to find Tommy Two Feathers. He grinned at Will.

'You come for Tommy?' He rolled his eyes. 'He busy right now.'

Will groaned. Tommy was a randy little bastard. He wondered what it was about Tommy that attracted the females.

'How long?'

Jontie considered.

'He be out back with Lisa, ten . . . fifteen minutes.' He nodded. 'You wait and have drink and then he be back. Right? You have drink on house!'

Will shook his head.

'Sorry, Jontie. No disrespect but I've got to keep a clear head. I know your moonshine and your habit of putting a snake in your beer. I'll pass on that but thank you. Another time, maybe?'

Jontie went back to his bar and served a very drunk Indian.

Will was getting impatient. He was in two minds about whether to go and break up what was going on the back room and drag Tommy away, when suddenly the door beyond the makeshift bar opened and a grinning Tommy emerged, buttoning up his trousers and obviously very drunk. He tossed Jontie a coin.

'That's for you, Jontie! Your wife's one of the best!' He came staggering over to the door, muttering about seeing to his horse and getting some shut-eye.

Then he saw Will. He tried to stand up straight and still, but swayed a little.

'Goddammit! What are you doing here?'

'Waiting for you!' answered Will grimly.

'What the hell for? We're not going nowhere!'

'We are, Tommy. We're off to California tomorrow, so you're going to have to sober up and be ready to ride!'

'Hell and damnation! I paid Lisa for tomorrow night! Goddammit! I can't go with you, Will!'

'Yes you can and you will!' Will wasted no more words over him but dragged him outside, to the interest of those watching.

Will headed for the nearest horse-trough and Tommy was in no state to fight him off. His head was held firmly down in the dank water until he gasped for breath. Three times, Will dunked him before letting up.

'All right, all right! Give over,' said a spluttering Tommy who was now trying to cough up more than just water. Will watched impassively as Tommy vomited. When, after a few minutes it was obvious that Tommy's guts were empty, he said quietly:

'You'll thank me in the morning, Tommy. Now come along and collect your gear and your horse. You're bedding down with me for the night. OK?'

Tommy only nodded. His head was still spinning.

Will looked at the little fellow and smiled. He was fond of the little runt. He was the best tracker in these parts, but that wasn't why Will was fond of him. He'd known Tommy's father in his youth. They'd been buddies, and when Frank took up with the Indian girl who had his baby, Will had been like a second father. When Frank had been killed, and the squaw had gone back to her tribe, Tommy, by then a young man of twenty years, had come looking for him. That had been six years ago. During his upbringing, he'd learned the secrets of the Cheyenne. He could track an animal or a man over stony ground and see what others couldn't see.

Tommy had become Will's secret weapon when riding the trail to California. He had a gift for sniffing out newcomers. Several times he had warned Will about advancing hostiles and Will never forgot that once Tommy saved his life when a young brave had crept up behind him and was actually wielding his war axe when Tommy shot him in the back.

The trouble with Tommy was that he was woman-mad and spent his spare time sparking the females. One of these days he would go too far and tread on some man's toes. He was always surprised that Jontie never took offence at Tommy cosying up to Lisa. But then, Jontie looked on her as a piece of merchandise to be exploited. What she earned went into his coffers.

He left Tommy, now thoroughly alert and awake, to get ready for the drive out. He had other business to attend to before this night was through. He needed his wagons to be overhauled. Two were already packed with ploughshares and several cases of guns and ammunition. They had been made ready to wait for the first drive in spring, but now his associates would get them all the sooner. He also had to have extra horses for the journey and spare axles in case the wagons broke down. He also had to let it be known that Will Hunter needed drivers again. The word would soon spread and there would be a stream of men willing to take a chance to go to California. Many of his drivers never came back to Abilene. It was a one-way ride for the itinerant drifters, and those who reckoned to find gold in the Californian gold-fields.

It was a long night.

He found time for a couple of hours' rest before the first rays of the sun came over the horizon. He took a hasty breakfast at his rooming-house and found Tommy up before him, with no sign of last night's drunken orgy. Will could only admire his ability to recover so quickly.

'So you managed to wake up,' taunted Tommy, stuffing the last of Mrs Malone's panbread in his mouth.

'Yeah, and you don't look so bad yourself considering last night!'

'That's because I got myself all cleaned out with Lisa!' Tommy chortled.

'Lisa be damned! You threw your guts all over the place after I dunked you!' Will laughed good-humouredly. Then he became grave again. 'Tommy, we've got a real job on our hands. You know the risk we're taking. You've got to lay off the booze and take it steady as we go.'

'Why do you say that?'

'Because there's three females travelling with us. That's why!'

Tommy's jaw dropped open.

'You mean to say there's three women travelling with us?'

'Yep, and they've no menfolk. Now listen . . .' He broke off for a moment as Tommy whooped and sprang to his feet. 'Sit down you randy bastard and listen!' and Tommy sat down again but now there was a gleam in his eyes. He was all attention.

'We've got to leave Abilene as soon as those folks show up. It's going to a risky trek and we're going to have to force-march. It'll be early mornings and late-night camping, and you and everyone else will have to be alert at all times. Now you, Tommy, I'm counting on you to assist the women as well as doing the usual scouting, and by God, I want you to watch the weather! You've got it in your bones to sense any change that's coming, and I don't want you drunk! So, no hidden bottles of liquor, d'you hear?'

Tommy nodded, now grave and understanding the situation. Still, for Tommy there were three rays of sunshine amongst the dark clouds.

Will checked his supplies. Thank God, he'd had the forethought to keep one of his wagons packed up with staples. He inspected his water-barrel which was fixed on the side of the wagon he would sleep in. It was infested with little worms. He pulled out the spigot, emptied the dregs of stale water, then hauled buckets of water from the well near the hostelry. He swilled out the barrel, then proceeded to fill it. It was important to fill the water-butts just before leaving on a long trek.

His drivers whom he'd recruited during the night gathered in the open space before the church and old Dick Randel brought in a small remuda of horses that he and Will had dickered over late last night. Will inspected them. Old Dick had kept his word and delivered good healthy stock. He was ready to ride.

It was a little after midday when the small cavalcade arrived in town. Will watched the straggly line, inspecting the wagons as they came. It was important that the wagons should be in good condition. A busted axle could put them back days and time was of the essence in this case.

Jack Broadbent was in the lead. He stopped beside Will, jumped to the ground and strode over, holding out his hand.

'Hi! Sorry to be a little late. Some of the womenfolk wanted to do some extra packing. You know what women are,' he said ruefully. 'Better to let 'em have their own way. Saves a lot of earache!'

Will grunted.

'Let's get this straight, Broadbent. In future the womenfolk will do as they're told! We're not on a summer outing. This trek could be a life or death job. Is that clear?'

'Of course. You made it plain, but there's no real danger, is there? After all, if there's a little snow, the Oregon trail will still be open!'

'We hit the Oregon Trail when we've covered a hundred miles and we join it at Fort Riley. Have you ever travelled along the Oregon Trail, Mr Broadbent?'

'Nope! But I understand it's a well-used trail with several forts along its route. We'd get plenty of help if we needed it!'

'That's what you think, mister. It's all of three hundred miles to the next fort and nearly five hundred miles to Fort Laramie because of the winding trail.'

'So when do we hit the Californian trail?'

'At Fort Caspar, about fifty miles beyond Fort Laramie. It's then that things could get tough. It's a winding trail over grass and desert and the mountains. I want to get over the mountains as soon as possible. If we get caught in the snow it would be impossible to travel. That's why we'll be pushing on as fast and as long as we can each day, and I don't want to hear any grumbles from the womenfolk. Right?'

'Aye, I'll tell 'em.' Rubbing his whiskery chin,

Broadbent walked along the little cavalcade and had a word with each man on the driving-seats.

Will gave him time and while he did so, made a point of introducing himself to Broadbent's woman. He saw two young boys peeping out of the wagon behind her.

'Hi! I'm Will Hunter, the man leading the wagon-train. Pleased to meet you.' He gazed into the sun-dried leathery-looking face of Lucy Broadbent. He noted the disapproving lips and the closed look. She appeared to be older than she really was. Too much working outdoors, Will reckoned. Probably Broadbent used her as some kind of pack-horse. 'Are these your sons?' he asked easily.

'Of course. Who else's would they be?' she asked in a truculent voice. He was taken aback at her tone, so just raised his hat courteously and walked on to the next wagon.

It belonged to the preacher and his short, fat wife, and their wagon was filled to the extreme. He wondered where they would sleep.

'Hiya, Reverend! Good to see you again!' He nodded at the little fat woman sitting quietly beside the preacher. She looked meek and rather lifeless, Will thought. 'Are you going to introduce me to your wife, Reverend?' he said aloud.

'Oh . . . ah . . . yes! This is Emma and my sons and daughter are in the wagon behind. I always travel with two wagons as I carry Bibles and hymn-books for the heathen. I find they are in great demand!' His large tombstone teeth glistened white in the sun. He was sweating and he took off his hat and fanned himself. 'You don't object to two wagons, Mr Hunter?'

'Nope! As long as you and your sons can manage them. I see you have no back-up horses, Reverend. Isn't that a risk?'

The Reverend Mordecai Logan raised his eyes to heaven.

'The good Lord giveth, and the good Lord taketh away! We are putting our faith in God. He will help and sustain us during this memorable journey. You'll see!'

'Then pray for us all, Reverend. We shall all need your prayers.'

He passed down the line and met Andrew Witherspoon, the storekeeper from Wichita who was aiming to try his luck with his goods in the gold-fields.

Further along was Mick Mayo, a man of forty and a former soldier. His face was hard, his eyes reflecting the harrowing scenes he'd seen in battle. Will reckoned this man would be useful if it came to fighting. He was tough and wore his guns low on his hips. A regular shootist: the gun in the boot by the side of the Conestoga wagon was an army repeating rifle and it was well-oiled and obviously part of the man himself.

'Hiya! I see you're well prepared.' Will nodded at the heavy wagon and the two extra horses tethered behind.

'Yeah, this old prairie schooner can knock hell out of the horses. I reckon to change them every twenty miles. It pays in the end. Gives 'em all a chance to recover.'

'You sound like a seasoned traveller. This is not your first long-haul trip?'

Mick laughed. 'I've been on long hauls all over the country.' He tapped the wagon. 'She's seen some mighty fine country and some of the most God-forsaken places! But everywhere I go I'm welcomed, and you know why?'

Will shook his head.

'No. You tell me.'

Mick tapped the wagon again.

'This old wagon carries what everyone wants, and those who're prepared to pay get what they want!'

Will frowned.

'You're telling me you're carrying guns and ammo?'

'Too right, I am, and dynamite too!' He grinned. 'Does that surprise you?'

'No. But the thought of you in the middle of my wagon train appals me. You will have to bring up the rear. I'm not having you blowing up amidst the rest of 'em!'

'You can ease your mind, mister. I've never

been blown up yet!' He leaned forward and waved Will nearer so that he could whisper. 'I'm a friend of Running Deer. You know, the rebel Indian who lives up in the hills. My only danger would be from a flaming arrow and Running Deer would see that that would never happen!'

'Goddammit! You're an Indian-lover!'

'Yeah, why not? They want what I tout and they pay what I want. I've no loyalty for the Yankees. They turfed me out of the army after the war with hardly a thank you. I've got to make a living!'

Will grunted. He too knew of men who'd survived the war but not the peace. He nodded.

'Just keep what you've told me to yourself. I don't know how the others will take it.' He looked meaningfully at the wagon drawn up behind Mick's.

Mick nodded. He'd already seen the two men on the wagon. A Negro who was driving and the rangy man beside him.

Will was reluctant to approach Lance Pritchard. He had no time for bounty hunters and this man looked hard and sinewy, as if the sun had dried him out. The cold blue eyes stared into his as if challenging him.

'Howdy! I see you're all set to go!'

Lance Pritchard grunted.

'And the sooner the better. I'll not rest until we're well on the way. This here feller is a slippery customer. Twice he's tried to cold-cock me but I've taught him a lesson he'll never forget!' He turned a cold contemptuous eye on the black man who was sitting hunched up and staring stonily ahead, the reins slack in his hands.

Then Will saw the whip-marks peeping from a torn shirt and there was caked blood on the man's hands. Will felt sick. He wanted to punch this cold, calculating bastard on the nose, but he only nodded and walked away.

He reckoned they might have trouble with that one before the trek was over.

He looked up and down the street. All his drivers were there ready and waiting, but where the hell was Billy? Then he saw him come lurching along the street leading his horse.

'You're late!' he snapped. 'You should have been here at dawn.'

'Why? You don't seem to be going anywhere fast!'

'That's not the point. You should have been here to help load up.' Then Will stopped and sniffed. 'By God, you smell like a skunk! I'm not having you driving my wagon and contaminating my staples with your stink! Here,' he pulled a wad of notes from his jacket-pocket and counted out twenty dollars, 'go to the store and buy yourself a complete set of clothes. Mind you get new underpants, and wipe your arse in future, and while you're at it, go to the barber's and get him to shave your head and your beard after you've had a bath! I want you back here in an hour and I want you smelling of carbolic soap. Right?'

'Hell! I'll get my death of cold if I bathe. I don't mind shaving but to strip naked . . .' Billy shuddered at the thought. 'Do I really have to bathe? I can't smell myself. I can't be too bad!'

'Billy, you haven't got my nose! If you don't come back smelling of carbolic then you don't ride with us! Take it or leave it!'

Billy growled some reply that Will didn't catch but he lurched away, leading his horse. Will saw him tether it in front of the store.

Billy was heading for a complete make-over.

Then he watched his wrangler leading in a herd of horses, all tied one behind other by their tails. He gave the man a wave.

'Hiya, Juan,' he called to the dark Mexican. 'Can you harness up two of them to that light wagon of mine? The one carrying extra water and the sacks of grain for the horses.'

Juan grunted. He was a man of few words, then he surprised Will by saying:

'I'll drive the wagon. I'll tether four horses behind and the others I'll rope on to the backs of your other wagons, if that's all right with you? I've got piles,' he said briefly.

Will nodded. It was one of the hazards of riding steaming horses for hours on end. He'd suffered himself in the past.

'That's OK by me, Juan. If you want salve, then ask Doc McLochry for some before we set off. He carries everything with him, does the doc.'

Juan nodded, still with a dour expression, and Will felt sorry for him. Every jolt of the wagon could be hell for him.

He had put off to the last the meeting with the women. They were drawn up a little away from the rest. He saw there was a young boy with them. Their driver, no doubt.

'Good morning ladies.' He raised his hat to them. 'All well and fighting fit, are we?' His eyes slid over them all, then lit on the boy. 'And who might you be, son?'

Betsy smiled at him.

'Oh, this is Pete. He's a bit . . .' She hesitated as the boy stared woodenly at Will. Oh, God, he thought, not an idiot! Then Betsy coughed. 'Pete's little bit . . .' She looked knowingly at Will and raised her eyebrows. 'But he's as strong as a bull and he won't let anyone come near us unless we want them to.' Then Betsy came close and said in a half-whisper. 'He's good with horses but he got a crack on the head and he's a bit . . . you know. But he won't be no trouble on the trail. We couldn't leave him behind. He's devoted to us all. I nursed him, you know, after his accident and he reckons he owes us. You wouldn't stop him from coming with us?'

Will looked at the buxom Betsy. She was a

good-looker and now she was watching him anxiously.

'I sure won't, ma'am. If you say he can pull his weight, then he's OK by me!'

'Oh, thank you, Mr Hunter, sir. It means a lot to us to have him with us!'

He smiled at her. 'Call me Will!'

Her eyes flashed and then she looked demurely at the ground.

'Thank you . . . Will. If there's anything I can do for you on the journey, you'll let me know, won't you?'

Will gazed into her eyes and felt his knees shake. Then he was brought back to reality by hearing the girls giggling behind him. He swallowed a lump in his throat.

'Yes, ma'am,' he managed to stutter. He thrust his hat more firmly on his head and stalked away.

Betsy watched him go and sighed.

'Now there goes a real man. I wonder if he's married?'

'As if you cared either way!' said Jenny pertly. 'It's never bothered you before!'

'You mind what you say, young woman!' Betsy snapped and heaved herself aboard her wagon. 'Are you both coming or not?'

Billy arrived back from the barber's. Will hardly recognized him. He was younger than he'd thought, not yet pushing thirty. His face and head were pale. He looked a bit piebald but the sun would soon even him up.

His checked shirt and denim trousers smelled new and his new boots creaked. He'd even bought a new black hat, and he grinned as he told Will the storeman had thrown in a used jacket that had been taken off a corpse by the undertaker and given to the storeman, who wanted rid of it.

'I also got an extra box of shells,' Billy said with some satisfaction. 'It appears that yon storeman isn't used to getting cash up front. Most folk put their goods on the slate and pay up when their cows go off to Chicago.'

Will grunted.

'At least you smell better!'

Billy laughed and fingered his chin and then his bald head.

'You know, I've not seen my face for years! It looks older, a stranger's face, and as for this dome, at least I haven't got a scalp-lock for those pesky Indians to get a hold of!'

'Right, and you'll have got rid of any lice you were carrying! From now on, keep yourself clean!'

Billy looked at him ruefully.

'You sound like my old pa! I was glad to get away!'

'So you joined the army, then?'

Billy looked startled.

'How did you guess?'

'Because of your reflexes with a gun and keeping those guns of yours cleaned and oiled. Are you a deserter, Billy?' There, it was out. Will looked hard at the young man. Billy scowled.

'Can I trust you? You're not going to call the sheriff?'

'Nope! I just want the truth. I want a driver, not some prisoner with the military sniffing at his heels!'

Billy took a deep breath.

'Look, Mr Hunter, I'll give you it straight. I killed a sergeant. He was beating up my buddie and I waded in and told him to stop. The son of a bitch lashed out at me and then everything went red and misty and when the smoke cleared and I could see again, he was lying at my feet, shot through the heart and I had my smoking gun in my hand. They charged me with murder but as the sergeant was a bastard with the men, I was given twenty-five years hard labour. My buddy helped me to escape but he was shot as we went over the wall together. There was no time to stop to see if he was dead or alive. I kept going, and that was months ago. I just want to get to California and start a new life. Is that so bad?'

Will looked at him hard but Billy did not flinch. Will reckoned he was telling the truth.

'Right. We'll say no more about it, but remember, no trouble on the trail!'

Billy watched him walk away. Now there was a guy he could follow for the rest of his life. He'd watch Will Hunter's back and woe betide anyone who tried to pull a fast one on him!

Will went to the head of the wagon train and mounted up on his horse, which Tommy Two Feathers was holding for him.

'One last chore, Tommy. Get back there and tell that Mayo, the one with the Conestoga wagon, to get out of line and bring up the rear, and then tell those womenfolk to take his place.'

'I can understand about the womenfolk. They need an eye on them, but why Mayo at the rear?'

'He's toting guns and ammo, Tommy. If we run into trouble, I don't want his wagon blowing up amongst the others. Savvy?'

'Gee, boss. We've certainly got a mixed batch this trip! Something tells me it's going to be mighty different from all the other trips we've made!'

Will agreed with him. If it wasn't for the extra cash, he would have called off the trip and to hell with them all, except of course, the womenfolk. He would never consign Betsy Goddard to hell!

THREE

They had been three days on the trail. Already there were grumbles at the forced pace. The womenfolk wanted to camp in the early evening so that they could cook and wash clothes if they were fortunate enough to find a good camping-site by a river.

Will Hunter remained firm.

'We're not on a Sunday school picnic,' he'd bawled at the men who'd been persuaded to come to him. Only one woman didn't complain. It was Emma Logan who rarely spoke and never had been known to air an opinion about anything. It seemed that the good Reverend spoke out for her at all times.

Then Will had gone on to give them a pithy account of what might happen if they dawdled along the trail.

The men were silent, then each one nodded gravely and returned to his wagon.

Betsy and her girls remained.

'Aren't you coming a bit strong, Will?' she asked. 'You're scaremongering. Look all around. There's not the first sign of the fall. We'll be well on our way before winter comes.'

'Betsy, you wouldn't like me to advise you on your own business, would you? You're the expert in your field. I'm the expert here. Doesn't that tell you anything?'

She made a face.

'Put like that, I expect you're right. It's just so tiring and we don't have time to bathe. I'm beginning to smell already!'

'But in the nicest possible way,' Will said gallantly and Betsy smiled at him.

'Thank you. You're very kind.' She turned to the girls. 'Come, Annie and Jenny, let's get back to the wagon.'

Another two days' drive brought them to Fort Riley and here they joined the main Oregon Trail. A small town had grown up outside the fort and the townsfolk looked on in astonishment when they heard that the wagon train was going all the way to Sacramento.

Crowds gathered and Betsy had several offers to stop at Fort Riley; even the sheriff was enthusiastic about her remaining with them, much to the disgust of the sheriff's wife who happened to be an onlooker at the time. Later she would give him hell.

They stayed long enough to take on further foodstuffs and Will learned that hostile Indians had been seen along the route.

The womenfolk ransacked the small store for women's fal-de-lals and Doc McLochry made a few dollars selling bottles of his made up elixir that cured all ills. Also, his dentist's chair came in useful as he had a small queue of people wanting a tooth pulled. All in all, he was satisfied with the stopover.

Then came the monotonous drive again, when weary and red-eyed with lack of sleep, all the men tried to keep alert against any marauders, either white or red.

Tommy Two Feathers rode ahead and scouted. He would come back wearily to eat at midday and report any movement, then ride away again in another direction. He would return, shaking his head and Will's heart was a little lighter. That night they would only need one watchman. The rest could catch up on their sleep.

Their next stop would be at Fort Kearny. There, Will would get first-hand knowledge from the fort commander of any hostile uprising and, if necessary, he could ask for an escort of troops to take them on to Julesberg which was the furthest outpost of the military at Fort Kearny. Of course he would have to pay the commander. It was the done thing. That way, the commander augmented his meagre pay and any wagon master would get protection. Will reckoned he could well afford what the commander would expect. At this time his spirits were high. Maybe that feeling of doom had only been imagination. Maybe the snows wouldn't come early in the mountains and they'd get by.

Each night when they camped, it became usual for the men travelling alone to meet at Will's fire and they would talk. Billy and the black man proved to be good cooks. Billy had been a chore-boy on a chuck wagon when his father had taken him on a cattle drive after his mother died. He'd helped the cook and picked up many tips. Abel too had been brought up to help at home when just a nipper. These two found much in common, especially when Billy confided one night after he'd been drinking from his private stash of liquor that he too had been a prisoner.

This was the time when Will would ask Tommy anxiously if he could smell bad weather coming and did he feel it in his bones.

Tommy's reply at this time was reassuring.

No, he saw no bad omens. The animals he'd seen weren't moving south. The wind was in the right quarter and the stars at night were clear and bright. He'd shaken his luck-bones which he carried in a small pouch around his neck and they'd fallen in a good pattern. There was nothing to worry about . . . yet!

It was a weary bunch of men who drove into Fort Kearny. There was no rejoicing, just a tired acceptance that they'd made it. Will's interview with the commander, Colonel Sloane, hadn't gone well. He'd been told he was a fool to set off on this journey and on no account would he provide an escort into enemy country at this time. He would have to travel on to Julesberg without his help. Not that there was trouble, he hastened to say.

'All is quiet at the moment. We reckon the Cheyenne have moved south to their winter quarters.'

So Will had become apprehensive again. The men protested when he told them there would be no stopover and no carousing in the one saloon of the little town that had grown up around the fort. They would be on their way. They would have time to change horses, check hoofs for wear and the wrangler looking after Will's horses would stay behind at the blacksmith and bring on any newly shod horses. Of course the wrangler would expect a small fee for doing so. This information was met most glumly. The men hadn't expected any hidden extras during the trip.

Andrew Witherspoon exploded.

'If we had a proper stopover, we wouldn't have to hire your wrangler! I didn't expect to have to pay extra!'

Will eyed him levelly.

'If your horses need shoeing, the only alternative is for you to pull out and then follow on behind. It's your choice, Mr Witherspoon.'

Andrew Witherspoon looked a little frightened.

'I don't fancy that. A lone man with a wagonload of goods! If there was anyone around, I could be dead meat!'

Will shrugged.

'That's what my wrangler would be facing. He'd be gambling with his life and that's what you would be paying for!'

In the end there were only four horses needing shoeing and the wrangler grinned at Will.

'Thanks, boss. I owe you. You put the fear of God into that feller! I didn't expect to get paid extra!'

Will laughed.

'Look, we're putting our lives on the line for these sons of bitches, so we make 'em pay!' Then his face changed and a worried frown was plain to see. 'I didn't reckon on the lack of an escort to Julesberg. It's going to be tougher than I thought!'

'We'll get through, won't we, boss?'

'Yeah. Don't worry about it. We'll make it!'

Andrew Witherspoon opted for the wrangler to see to the horses. So did the preacher and Hank Holden, who had two to shoe.

The wagon train moved on. Colonel Sloane watched them go, shaking his head and saying to his aide that that was the last time they would see Will Hunter.

Julesberg was a 300-mile trek and was situated about half-way to Fort Caspar, which was where the California Trail branched off from the Oregon Trail. They followed the Little Blue River for a while. It was tough going; the womenfolk grumbled and the men were beginning to look grim.

There were several unscheduled stoppages as wagons got stuck in deep ruts and one wagon had to have a new back axle. Will cursed the stoppages. It was time-wasting and they hadn't any to spare.

There were signs of the fall. Trees were beginning to turn colour. Grass was now dried hay and the nights were colder. The Reverend Logan's young daughter developed a cough and stayed huddled up in a blanket most of the time. It was with relief that they rolled into Julesberg and Will's drivers and Mick Mayo and Lance Pritchard went on a drinking-binge as a celebration of getting there without meeting up with the Cheyenne.

Will was furious. They were already three days behind schedule and after loading up fresh supplies he was ready to roll. He showed no mercy as he kicked his men out of their sleeping-quarters before dawn to get ready to ride. That morning every driver had a heavy hangover and Will reckoned that if they ran into the Cheyenne now it would be a massacre.

But they were lucky. Tommy Two Feathers, knowing the gravity of the situation, had laid off the booze. It had been a hard decision on his part but he knew the consequences if he'd taken at least one drink, and he reckoned his life was worth more than one drink. He left Julesberg just after midnight and ranged the trail for the next twenty miles. When dawn broke he realized that all was quiet. He had seen no Indian campsite or any signs that they had travelled the trail lately. He'd come back meeting up with Will a few miles out of Julesberg.

'All's quiet, boss. It's kinda too quiet. I don't like it. The Cheyenne don't usually leave their territory before they have to. I only saw a couple of small herds of deer and they were heading south.'

'You reckon we're in for a blow?'

'Could be. I reckon you should talk to the men and push on as fast as we can.'

Will nodded. He knew this was more than a hint. So that night, when they camped after a long day, he visited all camp-fires and spelled it out to the men, and the women, too.

'If we're to have any chance of reaching Sacramento, we've got to lighten the loads. Any of you folk carrying stuff that you don't need, then leave it behind. Dump it! Make your wagons as light as possible and change your horses regularly.'

There was a great outcry from the women.

'That's impossible,' cried Lucy Broadbent, who appeared to be the most forceful of the women. 'My grandather clock belonged to my mother and it's travelled with me wherever I've gone! I can't just leave it behind! She glared at Jack. 'Tell him, Jack! Go on, tell him!' Jack Broadbent looked at the ground and twisted his hat.

'Mr Hunter, you sure don't expect we'll leave an expensive clock behind? We didn't bargain for this. We're paying plenty!'

Will shrugged.

'You'll have to lighten your wagon, Mr Broadbent. I don't care what you leave behind, but lighten it you will!'

The men travelling alone were more reasonable and only Mick Mayo raised any objections. His wagons were carrying loads that couldn't be ditched. He would have to get rid of his own personal gear. It was reasonable that he couldn't dump guns and ammo. Again Will shrugged.

'It's up to you, Mayo, but don't ditch your grub. That's all I have to say.'

Emma Logan surprised him. The little plump woman was emphatic that she couldn't leave her iron stove or her heavy iron stewpot behind. Will had never heard her say much more than 'Good day, Mr Hunter' during the time they'd travelled together. The preacher gave him a big-toothed grin.

'She be a great one for the cooking. It's her life. It'll break her heart to leave her stove behind.'

'You'll have to persuade her, Reverend. She can keep the stewpot but the stove must go!' He sighed.

'The Lord giveth and the Lord taketh away! I'll see it's left behind.'

So when they moved on next day there were several dumped articles, among them a huge chest left behind by Betsy and her girls. It contained some treasured gowns and such things as fans and high-heeled shoes. Betsy had been very quiet when Will had visited her the night before but she wasn't going to get involved in any argument with this man. She had plans for him. Nevertheless, the loss of the chest was a great blow. It had taken years to gather together the gowns that she regarded as part of her trade.

The wagon train rolled on and soon the travellers realized why they had had to lighten their wagons. The trail became rougher than ever and they had to cross rivers and climb ever steeper gradients, so that much of the time they had to yoke extra horses on to the wagons.

Doc McLochry grew concerned about Reverend Logan's daughter, who was now coughing badly. Mrs Logan had begged him to come and look at her. She was now lying permanently in their wagon, unable to sit up and, what was worse, she was refusing food.

Will saw him leaving the Logans' wagon.

'Is the girl worse, Doc?'

Doc McLochry shook his head slowly.

'Much worse. I doubt she'll last more than a few days. She's going into decline. I think she's consumptive and she's into the last stages of it.'

'Can't you give her any of your medicine, Doc?'

The doc laughed bitterly.

'What good would that do? My medicine might be good for most ills but not consumption! What she needs is fresh milk and fresh vegetables and fruit, not this bilge we're having to live on! That man should never attempted to go on this trip! He must have known the danger she was in! It's monstrous! He puts me in mind of one of these fanatics who doesn't see or care what's going on around him. Look at his wife . . . she's browbeaten and anyone can see she's frightened of him. Then there's the sons. They act like cowed animals, and the younger boy looks consumptive too!'

'Maybe that's why he wants to get them to

California. The climate might be better for them.'

'Huh! Some hopes!' The doc stalked away to Will's wagon, which he was driving.

It took ten days to reach Fort Caspar and they were a tired, jaded lot. There were no celebrations in the small township.

Will took advantage, selling some of his freight to the local store and filling up the empty wagon with an extra water-barrel and dry-goods like coffee, flour and beans. He was thinking ahead about the stint over the mountain range when they turned away from the Oregon Trail and hit the California Trail. This was going to be the crucial time and he was dreading it.

They were now travelling in Wyoming. After leaving Fort Caspar the trail ran along by the Sweetwater River; the going was good and the women grumbled at having to leave some of their goods behind. They reckoned that Will was an old fusspot. Betsy rued leaving her chest behind but kept her mouth shut.

Several times she had talked to Will during their late-night camping. She'd given him plain hints of cosying up with her but he had only looked at her with appreciative eyes and tactfully told her that though he admired her and in other circumstances would have found it a pleasure to entertain her, he must now refuse. His mind was on this trip and on nothing else.

The going was good. Only the first signs of the fall showed and only Tommy Two Feathers watched for the turning of the leaves from shades of green to the golden-russet hues. Now, there was only a hint of the rich colours to come.

The men grew lax in their watchfulness. Even Will felt relaxed as he rode in front of the wagon that Eddie Doolan was driving. He heard Eddie whistling. Always a good sign when the erstwhile gambler was satisfied with his life.

Then suddenly his thoughts were shattered by a galloping horseman coming over the horizon at top speed. Will screwed up his eyes to see better and groped for his field glasses. His heart sank as he made out Tommy coming hell for leather, lying across his horse's neck. It was the old Indian trick of distributing his weight to make it easier for the horse.

Tommy met them head on and was out of the saddle as the mare pulled up in a cloud of dust.

'Boss,' he called, panting with exertion. 'There's a bunch of no-good Apache back there! They've raided a Comanche settlement to the north, and they're heading this way!'

Will swore.

'What in hell's got into them at this time of year? They should be on the way south by now!'

'They are, boss, but they're attacking and plundering as they go! They're taking everything that can be moved. Food, blankets, skins and even some of the young girls if they can catch them!'

'Then they'll not be travelling fast!'

Tommy shook his head.

'The young bucks will be riding fast and the oldsters will be doing the clearing-up and looking after the prisoners. A lightning raid and they move on and the mop-up party follows on. That way, the young braves count coup and also protect their own older members of the tribe.'

'So what do we do? We can't stand here jabbering about it! Have we time to get off the trail?'

'No sir! They'll track us down and the heavy wheel ruts will tell them that we're loaded up. We'll have to do as we've always done, draw the wagons into a circle and fight it out!'

'Right!'

Will turned and waved to the watching drivers. They knew what that circular wave meant. Zac and Eddie Doolan cursed. Immediately, they left the procession of wagons and turned into a wide circle. The rest of the wagons followed them.

The horses were corralled inside on a tethering rope so that they wouldn't panic and break free when the firing began.

Betsy jumped off her wagon and ran after Will. He pulled up, frowning at her.

'You shouldn't be on foot, Betsy. Get back aboard!' he roared.

'Wait! What's happening?'

'Can't you see? We're circling and that means trouble!'

Betsy looked horrified.

'You mean . . . Indians?'

'Yes. Now get back aboard your wagon. When the fun starts get down into the bed of the wagon and keep your heads down!'

'Oh, God! They'll kill us all if they catch us!'

'Now, Betsy, don't come all hysterical on me. I've enough to worry about without a screaming woman on my hands! If you must know, you've a better chance of survival than we men have! You might not like living as an Indian slave but it's better than dying!'

Betsy gave a little scream.

'Oh, Jesus! Not that!'

Will gave her a tight smile.

'Cheer up. I've come through a good few Indian raids and I don't expect to end my days here and now! So go and keep those girls of yours quiet, d'you hear?'

He rode on to supervise the placing of the wagons and to see that the openings between the wagons were barricaded with whatever could be found that was bulky enough in the wagons themselves. The men worked like maniacs and Mick Mayo opened a couple of cases of rifles. He handed them out and, grinning, he offered Will a small drum containing sticks of dynamite.

'Used dynamite before, Hunter?'

'Yeah, in the army.'

'Well, take this little lot. I've opened another barrel. Between us, we should be able to put the fear of God into these Indians! If they're youngsters who are coming at us, it's very likely they've never come up against dynamite! They'll think the Fire God's angry with them!'

That night there were no camp-fires. Everyone was awake and jumpy. When a tree-branch creaked in the rising wind the men grabbed for their rifles.

They ate cold pork that night and the left-overs of bread, but at least their bellies were full.

The Reverend Logan prayed, but the rest of the men jeered at him and he took cover in his wagon saying that God was punishing him for travelling with heathens. However, he made sure that his two boys knew how to load a gun. He reckoned that shooting Indians was no different from shooting rodents. Mrs Logan was told in no uncertain terms to remain in the wagon with their daughter who was now in a comatose state. The younger boy cried and his father slapped him and told him to pull himself together and stop whining. The elder boy kept his thoughts to himself while his father ranted but afterwards he comforted his sibling.

'Don't mind Father, Teddy. You've got me. I'll look after you!'

Jack Broadbent had his family well organized. Mrs Broadbent was loading extra rifles for her husband and two teenage sons. They were now sheltering under one of their wagons and had made themselves a good barricade out of sacks of oats and anything else solid that could be handled quickly. Now they waited, tired but alert.

The first sign of trouble came an hour before dawn. There had been no noise but suddenly there was the hiss of a speeding arrow with a burning tip into the canvas top of one of Andrew Witherspoon's wagons. At once the fire took hold and the flames shot up into the early-morning light in an orange glow.

Then the real battle began. The ululating screams of the attackers froze the blood of those who'd never heard an Indian battle cry. Dark figures with painted faces leapt out of the shadows as other Indians on horseback circled the stand of wagons. The men defending didn't know whether to concentrate on those who were bent on counting coup or the riders.

A bullet ripped through the preacher's canvas top, embedding itself in the still form of the reverend's daughter. She never made a sound and it was only later that her mother realized she was dead.

Abel tugged at his ankle chain and glared at Lance Pritchard.

'Undo me, for God's sake! Give me a gun. I can shoot as well as the next man!' He rattled his chain, his ankle showing a raw wound where it had chafed. 'You're a bastard, Pritchard, but I'm willing to defend this wagon!'

They were both crouched low behind the barricade Abel had made. He was now chained to a wagon-wheel. Pritchard took a haphazard shot at a screaming figure scrambling upwards over a mound of sacks. The man's face disintegrated into a red bloody mass and the body fell close by Abel.

Two more dark shapes appeared, scrambling hard to climb over their inadequate defence. Pritchard shot one and Abel, lunging forward as far as his chain would allow, punched the man in the face just as he was lifting a fierce-looking tomahawk that glinted in the morning light. That punch saved Pritchard's life.

Breathing hard, he sank his Bowie knife into the unconscious Indian's chest before he could recover from the blow.

Pritchard looked at Abel and grinned.

'I never thought you would ever save my life, Abel. Thanks for that!'

Abel grunted.

'It was instinct. I intended to save myself! Don't think I would save a bastard like you because I wanted to. No sir! It was me I was thinking of! Now what about that spare gun?'

Reluctantly, Pritchard tossed him the key to his chain, then handed over his spare rifle.

'You point that gun in my direction and it's the last thing you'll do,' he growled. He turned back and aimed at a passing rider on horseback. He had the satisfaction of seeing him tumble from his saddle and lie still.

Abel laughed. Quickly he freed himself and was soon shoulder to shoulder with Pritchard, firing as fast as he could load up.

Will, crouched down beside Zac and Eddie Doolan, became aware of firing coming from the next wagon, which the three womenfolk occupied. Then, as he loaded up his own weapon during a lull in the fighting, he saw Betsy handling a repeating rifle as if she'd used one every day of her life. The woman surprised him. She was nothing like what he expected a madam to be.

Then the next charge came and he forgot all about her. He concentrated on the business of holding back these wild-eyed bastards.

Then he remembered the dynamite.

If only he could throw a stick in the midst of a bunch of riders!

That was the trick, but how to get a bunch of Indians to ride together? Then he remembered the light cart holding the water-barrel and the feed for the horses. It was now empty, the sacks and barrel having become part of their defences.

It would be an easy matter to send out a runaway cart. The Indians would instinctively chase after it. It was worth a try.

Tommy Two Feathers listened to Will's plan. He had stripped off and was now wearing only a loincloth, and a red bandanna around his head. He could easily pass for one of the enemy. He volunteered to take out the cart. When he reached the nearest stand of trees he would dive for cover. Will thought it might work.

So, while the shooting went on, he and Tommy made an opening in the circle. Zac and Eddie rounded up two horses, with some difficulty as the horses were terrified by the mayhem going on around them. At last they were harnessed up and ready to go.

Then, with a wild yell, Tommy lashed the horses and the light cart shot forward, with Tommy standing upright and holding the reins with one hand and wielding the whip with the other. Tommy's race had begun.

There were yells from the Indians. They thought one of their own had successfully infiltrated the wagons, and those nearby turned and chased after it, shrieking with delight.

Will watched as the horsemen grouped together. He counted at least a dozen as he calmly lit his first stick of dynamite and threw it at the bunch of riders as they pounded past his line of vision.

At once there were screams and yells as the dynamite exploded, leaving a crater in the ground. Black smoke erupted and with it, body parts of both horses and men hit the sky.

Mick Mayo, seeing what Will had done, grinned and reached for his own sticks. He threw three in quick succession to make a diversion. One landed in front of the youth who seemed to be in charge of the group. He and his horse disappeared in the midst of the explosion.

Then came the silence, more sinister after the continual noise of gunfire and then the ultimate sounds of exploding dynamite. Ears ached. Everyone looked at everyone else. Was it over? Had those savage bastards had enough?

For a while they waited for the next sortie but none came and Will climbed up on to one of the wagons. He took a look around. All was still. There was no sign of hostiles. Then he saw movement in the scrub in front of him and he raised his rifle. If there was a sly son of a bitch coming in for a last vain attempt to count coup, he'd be ready for him. He raised his gun and aimed at the bushes, his trigger finger itching.

Then Tommy stepped out of the bushes, limping, and Will gave a great yell of delight and waved at him.

Tommy waved back but Will could see he was hurt.

'Zac,' he yelled 'Get out there! Tommy's

coming in and he's hurt!'

Doc McLochry was a very busy man. He suddenly found he was needed in a professional capacity. Tommy wasn't the only one he had to treat. Hank Holden was dead, scalped early on and with a great open wound in the chest. Three drivers were also dead. Abel watched the doc do his work. He would have to report Pritchard's death soon.

He thought of the last few minutes of Pritchard's life. He'd been shot in the stomach and his insides were dropping out. When Abel had turned to look at him after his first cry of agony it was to see Pritchard staggering and holding in his entrails. Then he'd sunk to the ground, screaming. Then he'd looked at Abel.

'Help me! For the love of God, put a bullet to my head!' Abel had just looked at him and turned away. Again, Pritchard had screamed at him to put him out of his misery. Abel remembered the feeling of triumph as he bent over his once-brutal jailer.

'Why waste a bullet over you? You're dead meat as it is!' He'd gone back to shooting Indians and closed his ears to Pritchard's tormented screams. Then at last Pritchard lay still and when the great silence came, Abel turned him over with his foot as if he was some stray dog he'd found lying dead in the dirt. He felt nothing but a cold satisfaction. That man would never again torture and make his living as a bounty hunter.

FOUR

A pall of smoke still lay over the camp. There was still much to do. Graves had to be dug and prayers for the victims had to be said. The Reverend Logan was in his element. He made the most of the situation by giving a long sermon after the burying.

He showed no outward grief about the loss of his daughter. His favourite expression was on his lips as he raised his eyes to Heaven. 'The Lord giveth and the Lord taketh away!'

Will was sick to his stomach at hearing that expression at every turn. Damn the man for a hypocrite, he muttered to himself as he and Tommy surveyed the damage and then took a look at the Indian corpses, seven in all.

Tommy squatted so that he could look at a scalp-lock tied to a loin-cloth, then he stood upright, turning grave eyes on Will.

'I reckon we got on the wrong end of a war

party. These are Apaches, not Cheyennes. Now why should these Apaches be in Cheyenne country at this time? That there scalp is a Cheyenne scalp-lock. I reckon this band was after our supplies for the main band. That doesn't sound too good, boss. The hunting must be poor.' He looked at the sky, now hazy with smoke. 'I reckon we should be moving on pretty soon. The Apaches will be back and with a bigger force. They'll want their dead and they'll still want our supplies!'

'Right! We'll have everyone ready to move on at daybreak!'

But it wasn't as easy as that. The men paying extra for their guide to California reckoned they had a say in when and how they would travel. They still did not realize just how grave the situation was.

In vain Will pointed out that horses had to be fed and the stocks of grain were disappearing fast. Their own stocks of food were also going down and he warned everyone to go easy on the rations. He especially talked to the women about only cooking enough food for their requirements and to waste nothing.

There was much grumbling and Will was accused of being a doomsday Job. Only Eddie Doolan and Zac and the doc realized the true situation. They had been over the mountains to California many times and the going was always hard even in the best of times. They looked at each other and got on with the chores. They and the wrangler had the horses looked over and made ready to ride.

Andrew Witherspoon's wagon containing his food supplies had been fired and he was now having to rely on his neighbours for food. Hank Holden's wagon had also suffered fire damage, and Will thought ruefully, there was one less to pay up the extra cash when they got to California . . . if they got to California.

But on examining the blackened and half-burned-out wagon Will got a surprise. No wonder Holden had been prickly about his reason for going to California. Will found a chest hidden under the flatbed of the wagon. When it was broken open it contained not only gold coins but a newspaper and a Wanted poster of the man who had carried out the bank raid on a Wichita bank. Holden's real name had been Ned Bridges.

Ned Bridges! Even Will had heard of the notorious Ned Bridges! Tommy was with him when he made the discovery. He looked hard at Tommy.

'Not a word of this to anyone. Right!' Tommy nodded, grinning so much he nearly split his face in half.

'Too right, boss. This little lot could be just for you and me, boss. What d'you say?'

Will nodded, wishing Tommy hadn't seen the hoard. Not that he grudged splitting the contents, but Tommy was his own worst enemy. When he got drunk he couldn't keep a secret. Will knew Tommy had a low estimation of himself and he would brag about anything to think himself big.

He reckoned it wouldn't be long before everyone knew of Hank Holden's haul. He grabbed Tommy by the throat.

'Be sure you're not the blabbermouth, Tommy!' he said, between clenched teeth. 'If you've got a hidden stash of booze in your warbag, then keep it there! For as God's my witness, if you say one word about this little lot, I'll cut your tongue out! God rot me if I don't!'

'Aw, Will, don't be like that,' Tommy rubbed his bruised throat. 'I'd be a fool to tell anybody about this lot! It's the best chance in the world for me to become a wagon-train master. I'd buy me a wagon and trade goods and I'll be all set for a good future!' He grinned at Will. 'Just as you did when you were my age.'

'Well, keep that in mind, Tommy. If there's a sniff of what's in that chest, there could be mayhem amongst the others. That Billy for one, and the gunrunner for another. Both of 'em are unknown quantities and I sure don't want to wake up one morning with my throat cut and some bastard making off with the whole caboodle!'

Tommy crossed his heart and promised earnestly to keep his mouth buttoned up, but Will reckoned he'd have to watch the boy at night when they camped. God, didn't he have enough to worry about besides Tommy and that chest of gold?

He waited until late that night to remove the chest and hide it in one of his own wagons. It wasn't easy to camoulflage it under a pile of sacks but he managed it. Taking a look around he saw that the man on guard had been snoozing by the fire, his gun loosely held in his hand. Will reckoned he should give the man a good kick in the ribs now the job was done. He kicked out with his foot.

'Wake up, you lazy son of a bitch!' he yelled. The man jerked awake and grabbed for his weapon.

'Wha . . . what is it? Are we being attacked?' He blinked and tried to appear alert. 'I wasn't asleep, boss. I was only giving my eyes a rest. I swear it, boss!'

'Then did you see that coyote come sniffing around the camp ten minutes ago!'

The man looked up helplessly at Will.

'A coyote?'

'Yeah, a coyote. Why didn't you shoot it? It was as near to you as I am now.'

The man gulped.

'Gee, I must have dropped off after all, boss. I sure didn't know I was that close to the critter!'

'Then don't fall down on guard duty again, mister, or it will be the last time you ever drive for me!'

Will stalked off, a little grin on his lips. At least he knew that the man hadn't seen Will's furtive shifting of the chest.

For all Will's bellowings and bawlings it was three days before they got back on the trail. Already the vultures were flying high above them, having smelled the stench of rotting flesh from many miles away. The birds would come down as soon as the last wagon got under way.

Tommy scouted the country again and only once saw in the distance a dust cloud that denoted the movement of men. He waited and watched but it turned out to be a platoon of soldiers riding away from them on business of their own.

Will took heart at the news. If there were hostiles about they were keeping out of range at this time for fear of the soldiers. He could relax a little.

The younger men organized a hunting party to overcome the boredom of riding the slow wagons day after day. Sometimes they came back tired but with no luck, reporting that game was scarce. But twice they came back loaded with a kill: once a lone deer which had been lame and another time they came back with a half-grown deer and a brace of jackrabbits, all most welcome. Fresh meat was a luxury these days.

Will was beginning to think that their chances of making it were now doubled. They'd left Fort Bridger behind and opted for the shorter route by going on to Salt Lake City in Utah and travelling the trail that ran alongside the Great Salt Lake itself. This was the most gruelling part of the trail, for now they were approaching the dreaded foothills and the horses had to be changed many times for the wagons were now a dead weight. Most wagons needed four horses, but some, like Mick Mayo's wagons, which were laden with heavy guns, needed six horses to a wagon.

The wrangler was getting increasingly worried. He was running out of ready-made shoes for the horses and the sacks of grain were nearly exhausted. All the horses were getting about only a quarter of their rations and were now relying on the sparse grass.

Suddenly the nights were getting much colder. Betsy reported a film of ice on her water-butt and now she wore a blanket over her woollen shawl to keep out the cold. The girls complained and Will told them in no uncertain terms to wear all the flannel petticoats they'd brought with them all at once and to hell with the washing!

Tommy offered to sleep between the two and keep them both warm at night, but Betsy slapped him and told him if he wanted to keep anyone warm it would be her! Tommy pulled a face behind her back and later whispered to Will that if he was cold of a night he should take up Betsy's offer before someone else did.

Abel had joined up with Billy the Goat, now that he was free of Lance Pritchard. Will watched them both but they gave no trouble and Will came to rely on them to take over cooks' duties. Billy's hair had grown back but his beard was now clipped and in good order. He smelled a little, but it came from his feet rather than his body. His body odour was no worse than that of any of them, Will included.

There was no bathing at this time. Water was becoming scarce as they climbed higher into the mountains. Will noticed that the snow-line was now further down the mountainsides than he'd usually noticed at this time of the year. The snow was already falling beyond the tree-line.

It was a sign to put an extra spurt on. Again the men grumbled. They were moving at a gruelling pace already and the horses were looking gaunt. One animal had already dropped in his traces and had had to be cut free while the other animals lunged and kicked. It had taken several men to hold them until another horse was harnessed.

At each emergency stop the Reverend Logan insisted on a prayer-meeting, which angered Will. The preacher insisted that it was due to his prayers that they had succeeded in getting this far so safely.

'Believe in the Lord and he will take you under his wing and uphold you,' he would drone on, and yet, as a man, Will knew him to be a bully with his own family.

His younger son was sickly, yet Logan would not have it.

'He's just a lazy young layabout!' he would mutter when Will remonstrated with him about giving the kid jobs to do that he wasn't capable of.

'Why not let your elder boy do the heavy chores?' he asked heatedly one day when he found the younger boy carrying a heavy load of logs that had him bent nearly double.

'Because that lad's got guts! He doesn't need discipline! He drives my other wagon and I want him fit to do that, and might I remind you that it's none of your business how I treat my sons!'

Will had shrugged and walked away, but several times later on he'd helped the boy feed the horses and carry water for them without the boy's father knowing.

But one morning, after a particularly cold night, Mrs Logan gave a piercing cry that had everybody up and out with drawn guns. Betsy who was in the next wagon to them, ran to her. Mrs Logan was shaking.

'What is it, Emma?'

The Reverend Logan opened the canvas flap and looked out of the wagon. He stared coldly at Betsy.

'Will you keep away from my wife. And don't call her Emma in that intimate way! We don't want your kind contaminating us!'

Emma Logan turned tear-stained eyes to him:

'But, Mordecai, she can help me! What about Teddy!' she broke into fresh sobbing and Betsy, setting herself against the preacher's wishes, held her close.

'What about Teddy?' she whispered, and Will, who was coming to see what the ruckus was, heard her say in a wailing voice:

'He's dead! My Teddy's dead!'

Will looked up at the white-haired preacher who stood grimly there with no emotion on his face.

'Is this true? Is the boy dead?' The father showed no grief but nodded, and turned and went back inside the wagon.

The burial was private. Billy and Abel offered to dig a grave in the hard ground. Betsy stayed with Mrs Logan until the time came for the boy's burial and then she retired to her own wagon. There were only Mrs Logan and the remaining brother to listen to the preacher's prayers. Billy and Abel stood a little way from them until the time came to fill in the grave. No one felt the need to mourn for the boy. Everyone was of the same opinion: that the boy was better off where he was now than with his bullying father.

The wagon train moved on.

The days passed and now there were flurries of snow that laid in crevices among the rocks. The wind blew from the north and each night was now an ordeal. More fires were lit at night, even though there was the risk of hostiles locating them. Tommy scouted and found no movement of man or beast, and not even a new set of foot- or hoof-prints. They were now high in the wild country. They had left the last small outpost behind. Ahead was the mountain range. Soon they would be in the Sierra Nevada. The last great haul before they dropped down into the plains below.

The going got tough. Several more horses dropped in their tracks. Now Will considered cutting the best portions of the meat and eating it, to save their dried jerked beef for later. Betsy was horrified at the idea.

'I've never eaten horse in my life!' she cried, 'and I'm not starting now!' She wasn't the only one to protest. Broadbent's wife agreed with her. She'd never cooked horseflesh before and she wasn't starting now. Even Andrew Witherspoon tackled Will about it.

'Is it so necessary, Will? They're scraggy beasts anyway and will be as tough as leather.'

Will looked at him in a kind of rage.

'Look around you, man. You see that snow? Soon, it will be feet deep and not inches. We're not making time fast enough to get through this range and back down into the foothills. You lost your food supplies and you're living on your neighbours' good will. Now if we get bogged down—'

'Hell! You've moaned on about that all the way along the trail and nothing's happened yet! We'll get through. We've come most of the way. We'll soon reach Fort Churchill and then we'll soon be home and dry, so lay off, man. You only frighten the womenfolk!'

'Suit yourself, Witherspoon, but me and my boys are going to eat horseflesh as long as it lasts.'

Will walked away and went to supervise Abel and Billy about what had to be done. Fortunately, Abel had been used to slaughtering cattle, so he and Billy got down to the business of slicing off the best parts of the rumps. The rest would be left for the birds.

That night, Will and his drivers ate well. They had a huge stew made of horse-meat and chilli beans flavoured with dried herbs that Will had had the foresight to bring with him. He knew how monotonous grub on the trail could be. The smell of the cooking stew drew the attention of the other more finicky travellers. Eventually Mick Mayo came to squat down beside them.

'Any chance of a plate of that there stew?' He grinned disarmingly. Billy handed him a plate and didn't say a word. Will gave him a long straight look.

'Next time, when one of your horses founders, remember us!'

Mick nodded.

'You bet! It's not bad when you're hungry enough!'

Later, Mick was to remember that remark when he was so hungry he would have eaten a skunk.

The wagons lurched on their way. The gradient got steeper. Now, the families didn't need telling to shed heavy goods to lighten the loads for the starving horses to pull. A wooden chest was left behind, a crate containing treasured china was left at the wayside. A heavy metal bath was heaved overboard and Will smiled to himself. These folk were learning!

Then, one morning, they all awakened to find their wagon wheels half-submerged in soft snow which was steadily drifting. It clung to the pine-trees, turning them into ghostly shapes. A hazy blue mist encompassed everything and the water in their barrels was turning to ice.

It took a whole morning for all the men to dig a way out of the drifting snow. The wagons moved on for a quarter of a mile that day.

Then came the nightmare. Each day the exhausted men had to dig out a path for the wagons, until at last the covering of snow overcame their efforts and they were at a standstill.

Will knew his forebodings were coming true.

Doc McLochry was fast running out of medicines and bandages. There had been a flurry of injuries and one man was cut badly when his numbed hands slipped as he chopped logs, the axe biting into his leg.

There had been a run on his cough mixture as the icy air attacked lungs not used to the severe cold. He was a very worried man and more so when he realized his hidden stock of rotgut whiskey was about finished.

Tommy was sent out to find the way station that Will remembered from earlier occasions. It should be a few miles ahead if the Indians hadn't burned it down. Now, if it was still in existence, it would be shut down for the winter. There was hope yet for the travellers.

It was an anxious time waiting for Tommy to return. If he returned, Will thought pessimistically. The boy could have ridden into a hidden crevice in the rocks and that would be the end of him. So it was a great relief when Tommy came in. He was drooping over the neck of his horse.

Will rushed to help lift him to the ground. The boy was suffering from hypothermia.

'Tommy! Don't go to sleep, Tommy!' Will shook him. Tommy opened his eyes wearily.

'Is it you, boss? I thought I was done for! I guess it was the horse that brought me back. Good old horse. . . .' He sank back in a stupor. Will shook him again.

'Come on, Tommy! Liven up! No time for sleep.' He looked around helplessly and caught sight of Doc McLochry. 'Doc, bring us some of your rotgut. That'll bring him round!'

Doc sighed. He only had half a bottle left but, looking at the boy, he knew Tommy's need exceeded his own need. He went and fetched the bottle and watched as Will poured the liquor down the boy's throat. Some of it dribbled down his chin and the doc swallowed convulsively at the waste of good liquor.

Tommy shook his head, and coughed, and then managed to stand up straight.

'What about the shack, Tommy? Did you find it?'

Tommy's eyes opened wide as he remembered.

'Yeah, it's still there. At the rate we're travelling, it'll take us two days to get there!'

Will could have whooped with joy. At least they would have shelter.

The wrangler took charge of Tommy's horse

and Tommy was lifted into Will's own wagon, wrapped in Will's blankets and laid on Will's makeshift bed. Last night's stew was reheated and Tommy ate ravenously. Then he was allowed to lie down and sleep after Doc looked him over for frostbite. The boy was lucky, Doc opined. A few more hours and he would not have made it.

The digging and clearing of the trail went on. At long last the old shack, half-buried in snow, came into view.

A great cheer went up from those at the head of the train and, with a burst of new energy, the weary men made it.

Will counted the spare horses as they were turned into the corral next to the shack. Less than half of the number they had set out with. Soon, if things went on as they were now, there would be no spare horses for the wagons. Time would tell. Will reckoned those who had more than one wagon would have to face the fact that one wagon must be left behind. It would be hard but it had to be done if they were to reach Sacramento.

The shack was divided into three rooms, the largest being used as a bar and eatery. There was a pot-bellied stove and around it were arranged several rough tables and chairs. Two barrels and a roughly split pine-plank served as a bar. The shelves behind were now empty except for a few stained mugs. It was a cheerless place but now very welcome.

The two rooms behind were obviously a store-room and a combined living- and sleeping-room for the proprietor. It held a cot, an empty chest and a gun rack on the rough pine-log wall.

Will looked around; not much space for one family, never mind the rest of the travellers. This room would have to be given over to Betsy and the two girls if they had to stay there for any length of time. The rest would have to sleep in their wagons and come into the main room for food and shelter during the day.

He visited the outbuildings, hoping that some of last season's hay remained. There were a few musty bales in the stable, which he reckoned was better than nothing.

The blacksmith's shop fared better. There was still a small amount of iron, ready to be turned into horseshoes. A small stack of logs had also been left behind. At least they could be used to get the old pot-bellied stove going. The men would have to forage in the snow for extra supplies, which would have to be cut and dried before they would be of use.

Will was in no doubt that their stay might be protracted if the weather worsened. He looked up at the sky, trying to predict the weather to come. The wind was coming from the north, always a bad sign. He said nothing, however. He would wait. No need to panic these unseasoned travellers. Only Doc and Eddie Doolan and Zac knew all the signs and still they did not know what Tommy Two Feathers did . . . that the easing up of the snow meant one thing: that a greater storm was brewing.

The Broadbents and the Reverend Logan were much more cheerful, and even Betsy reckoned they were lucky to luxuriate before a pot-bellied stove that was now giving out warmth. Being under a roof made them feel that life was becoming normal again. Betsy wished she'd had one of her saloon dresses to change into, to give the illusion that they were back to normal times. She hated herself in the clumsy thick clothes she wore, topped up by a man's jacket and a blanket about her shoulders. It wasn't feminine. It wasn't fair!

Tommy was now recovered from his ordeal but had been told by Will to take it easy, for later on he would have to ride out and try and make Fort Churchill, which was a week's ride on a good horse. Will reckoned they would need help from the military to get through these mountains if bad weather really closed in on them.

Billy, a little miffed at Tommy's remaining idle while he and Abel laboured and helped to bring in logs for the stove and did the cooking as well, came to him one night when all his chores were done.

'Tommy, I want a word with you.'

Tommy eyed him speculatively.

'What about?'

'After you supped off the doc's booze you talked a lot of drivel. I was the one who tucked you up in bed. Remember?'

'Yeah, vaguely. I know someone heaved me into bed. So it was you, eh?'

'Yeah, and you were giggling at one point before you passed out and you were talking about gold. What was all that about, Tommy?'

Tommy's expression became guarded.

'I don't know what you're talking about. What gold?'

'That's what I'm asking you. Why babble about gold and knowing where it was hidden? Come on, Tommy, spill the beans!'

'Jesus, Billy. I don't remember anything about hidden gold! I must have been hallucinating!'

Billy lunged for him in a sudden fury and shook him.

'Don't give me that bullshit, Tommy! You know something and I want to know it too! Come on, give, or I'll choke it out of you!' He began to squeeze Tommy's neck and the little feller tried vainly to unlock Billy's grip on him. But Billy's shoulders and arms had been developed by breaking rocks in the penitentiary quarry before he'd made his escape.

Tommy gasped and spluttered and eventually gave in.

'All right, you bastard. I'll tell you, but it won't make any difference. If you got hold of the chest you wouldn't be going anywhere with it!'

'Well, where is it? Come on, talk or else!'

'That feller, Hank Holden who was killed—'

'Yes, what about him?'

'He was Ned Bridges, the bank robber!'

Billy whistled. He knew all about Ned Bridges but had never met him. He was one of the men most revered in the pen for his exploits.

'You mean Holden was Bridges? How come you know?'

'I was with the boss when he looked over Holden's wagon and he found the chest stashed under the wagon-bed. There was this chest and some newspaper cuttings and a Wanted poster. It was Bridges all right!'

Billy whistled again.

'So I reckon Hunter's got the chest hidden somewhere in one of his wagons,' he said softly. 'I wonder which one?' He frowned and looked hard at Tommy. 'You know which one?'

Tommy shook his head.

'I swear on my mother's grave, I don't know which one. The boss didn't trust me that far I reckon!'

Billy nodded, then suddenly seized Tommy again and shook him.

'Mind you don't go running to Hunter about me knowing about the chest, you hear? If you do and he comes for me . . . you're a dead man!'

Tommy blinked. He might be good at tracking and sensing changes in the weather but he was no fighting man when it came down to personal brawling. His idea of fighting was to creep behind an unsuspecting victim and put a knife in his back. He cowered low. Billy tossed him aside like a bundle of rags. He leaned forward over Tommy and giving him an evil smile, passed his fingers across his throat in a gesture that left nothing to the imagination.

Tommy gulped and watched Billy walk away. Now he was in a hell of a pickle. If he didn't warn the boss about Billy and his obvious intentions, he would lose his share of the gold, and if he did warn the boss, he could lose more than the gold. He could lose his life.

Life was hell.

FIVE

The worst storm for ten years hit them without warning. Intermittent flurries of snow had come down at intervals for the last two days and Will had viewed the drifting snow with concern. Several of the younger men had gone hunting but had come back exhausted and with nothing to show for their efforts. It seemed the animals had all migrated south. Even the continued search for dead wood was now hazardous.

Will gave orders that just one fire should be lit and that was in the pot-bellied stove. The women grumbled. How could they do their cooking alongside Abel and Billy? The answer was that their contribution of food was to be given over to the two men and everyone would share the results. Betsy and Lucy Broadbent pulled faces. They didn't like such as Abel and Billy to be in charge. What if they spat in the stew?

That remark brought down a whole heap of

trouble for the women and they were told sternly to keep their thoughts to themselves. Didn't they yet understand the situation they were in?

The storm came late at night. A crack of thunder awakened all those not on guard duty, and the lightning lit up the wagons and the shack with an eerie blue glare. Later, when the thunder had rolled away there came a silence so hair-raising that Eddie Doolan and some of the other older men heaved their blankets aside and stepped down from their wagons. They were appalled at the depth of snow now surrounding them.

The old log cabin was half-buried. Snow covered the small window which had been a storeroom. Jack Broadbent made his way with difficulty, ploughing through the soft virgin snow to reach the shack.

'You all right in there?' he bawled.

Betsy, with a blanket about her shoulders opened the door cautiously.

'Yes, apart from the girls being frightened to death at the thunder and lightning. What's happened? It's gone quiet!'

'Keep indoors, ma'am and keep that stove burning. And if I was you I'd keep a full pot of coffee boiling. I guess we're going to need it!'

Will, who had gone to look over the horses in the corral at the first crack of thunder, came by.

He looked cold and was shivering badly. Jack looked at him with concern.

'You been up all night, Will?'

'Yeah. Someone had to watch over the horses. We've lost two. They panicked and tried to jump the fence and broke their legs.'

Jack was appalled.

'Soon we won't have any spare horses!'

Will gave a wry grin.

'That's the least of our troubles. The way things are, we won't need spare horses! I'm on my way to find Billy and Abel. I want them to bring in the carcasses before they get covered up by snow. We're gonna eat those beasts and to hell what those finicky folk think! You know, Jack, we're running short on supplies. It was a big blow losing Andie Witherspoon's grub wagon.'

Jack Broadbent looked grave.

'We'll get through, Will. We've come this far, we can't fail now!'

Will sighed and stretched. His bones ached with the cold.

'It all depends on the weather and how we all pull together! From now on, we're going on short rations. No waste. Pass the word, Jack, that all jerked beef and pickled pork must be saved until after we eat these here horses. Cut up into joints, there should be enough meat to last a couple of weeks at least.'

Jack looked at him with horror.

'A couple of weeks? Jesus, we won't be here in a couple of weeks?' He looked about him and up at the sky which looked crystal-clear. 'It looks as if the worst of the storm is over. Surely we can dig our way out of here? We can't miss the trail . . .' His voice dwindled away at Will's expression. 'You don't think we can travel! It's the horses, isn't it?'

'Partly. They're weak and undernourished. We've got through a hell of a lot of grain for those beasts and we've more empty sacks than full ones! Besides, those low-bed wagons weren't built to move through three feet of snow!'

'Then what the hell are we going to do? We can't stay here for ever! We'd starve to death!'

'Now you've got the picture, Jack. I'm depending on an easing-up of the weather. When Tommy says there's a chance of making it to Fort Churchill I'm gonna send him. A platoon of soldiers hacking their way along the trail is the only solution I can see. Tommy might get through because he knows the country and can take short cuts on horseback.'

'You reckon he could do it?'

'If any man can, he will.' But Will wasn't as sure as he sounded. Would he be sending Tommy to a frozen death?

Eddie Doolan arranged a card-school to while away the time. It kept some of the gamblers amongst the drivers occupied. There were fewer quarrels over the three women. At first, the men were intrigued at having three whores amongst them. Betsy had proved very selective but there had been some fun with the two girls. But as time passed, the men's libido weakened. They were more concerned with keeping warm and surviving in that ghostly white wilderness. The trees had taken on grotesque shapes. Now they appeared to the men's imaginations as snow-covered ships. Branches, with their long streamers of snow and icicles, appeared like ropes or tentacles. It was now a white alien world with weird blue shadows, and at noon that same snow shimmered and glistened.

The men were now reluctant to forage for wood for the stove. One of the old outhouses was dismantled and the wood sawn up. It was easier than struggling through waist-high snow for frozen deadwood.

The Reverend Logan prayed daily. He reckoned all this would not have happened if they hadn't brought those loose women with them. It was a judgment on them all. He treated the women with contempt if he came face to face with them. His wife Emma, looking thinner and drawn, rarely left their wagon. The good reverend did not like her coming in contact with the men. Their remaining son came to the shack for their rations of food but rarely stopped to talk. He was sullen and downcast. He was served by Abel and Billy and then ignored.

Few members of the party gathered to hear Mordecai Logan's prayers and exhortations. His hell-fire preaching had made him unpopular and so, as he realized that his words meant nothing to his fellow travellers, his anger grew and he would bawl and shout, cursing those whom he felt responsible for their situation now. Most of his anger was against Betsy and her girls. It became so bad that Will had to take him on one side and explain a few facts of life to him. The reverend stared at Will.

'And who do you think you are to question my beliefs. Me, a man of God? All this,' and he waved a hand around at the scene before them, 'is God's way of showing disapproval. He is showing his might and his wrath! We must all kneel down and pray with the same mind and ask forgiveness of our sins. Only then will he relent and let us go on our way!'

Will looked at him with pity.

'You really believe that, don't you, Reverend.'

Mordecai raised his eyes to heaven.

'The Lord giveth and the Lord taketh away!'

Will was sick of hearing those words. It was as if they were Logan's creed.

'You're mad, Reverend. You're not in the real world at all! You're somewhere up there in space! I pity you. It seems as if your God is punishing you as well as all of us! What sins have you committed, Reverend?'

The preacher stared at him.

'I am God's mouthpiece. I am not a sinner!'

Will spat in the snow and laughed incredulously.

'You don't reckon the loss of your son and daughter a kind of punishment?' He didn't wait for an answer but walked away from the man in disgust.

Another three days dragged by and it was with growing concern that Will viewed the empty sacks of grain that had been the horses' mainstay. He saw with dismay that two more horses were in a bad shape. Soon there would be no spare horses for the wagons and perhaps not even enough horses to pull all the wagons.

The time might come when all the travellers and he himself would have to decide which wagons had to be left behind. It was time to consult Tommy. He had to make the great decision and send Tommy to Fort Churchill. He was their only hope.

Tommy looked grave when Will tackled him.

'How about it, Tommy? Do you think you have a chance?'

Tommy rasped his chin and looked at the clear sky and the watery sun, which was glinting down on the white world.

'If I can reach the pass, there would be a

chance, but there's another four hundred miles or so. Down on the plain, the going will be easier. Most of the snow will be gone. If I can take an extra horse?'

Will looked worried.

'We can't really spare one, but if you go, you'll have the extra one you want and it'll be the fittest we've got. It's important you get through, Tommy. Not just because it's your life, but it's all our lives too. You've got a great responsibility on your shoulders, Tommy and I'll hate to see you go. I think of you as a son, Tommy.' He clasped Tommy to him, his heart swelling up. He wasn't a very emotional man but Tommy was special.

That was the morning the rations were cut. Bread-portions were halved and the coffee as weak as water. Will came and instructed Billy to load Tommy up with all the jerked meat, bread and whatever was at hand that he could safely carry on his spare horse. Billy looked at Tommy as they were packing the loads.

'So, you're getting out of here. Any chance you'll make it?'

'Of course. I wouldn't be going if I didn't expect to get to Fort Churchill.'

'Then I'm coming with you,' whispered Billy, 'and you know why!'

Tommy looked horrified.

'Billy . . . you'd never rob Will Hunter! He's the one man who's given you a chance! You're on the run and he knows it! You wouldn't dare—'

'I'm not robbing him!' Billy broke in roughly. 'That gold wasn't his in the first place! I'm coming with you, Tommy and that's it. If you keep your mouth shut, we'll split what's in the chest. Right?'

'And if I don't keep my mouth shut?'

Billy leaned nearer and soke softly.

'I'll come after you and I'll slit your throat from ear to ear!' His eyes sparkled. 'It won't be the first time I've slit a man's gizzard!'

Tommy blenched. He was a scout, not a fighting man. He knew he would have no chance at close quarters with the burly Billy. He would have to think of ways of disarming him. Make him think that everything was OK. He nodded.

'You say you'll split fifty-fifty?'

Billy grinned.

'Yeah, my word's my bond!'

Tommy noted the grin. The bastard would rely on Tommy to lead the way to Fort Churchill and then, when they sighted the fort, Billy would expect to jump the unsuspecting Tommy and backshoot him. He could read Billy's mind like a book.

He smiled and reached out a hand for Billy to shake.

'Right. I'll take your word for it. I'd sure rather have you as a friend than an enemy!'

'When do you go?'

'Daybreak. Have the coffee ready an hour before dawn.'

Billy whistled when Tommy walked away. He now had his own plans. Sometime after midnight he would search Hunter's wagons and find that chest, stash it away near where his own horse was tethered in the makeshift stable, grab a bag of oats and be ready to ride when he saw Tommy on his way. He faced the fact that he needed Tommy to lead him out of this hell-hole. Without Tommy he'd have no chance. He whistled as he worked around the camp and Abel wondered why he was so cheerful.

'What you so perked up about, Billy?' Abel asked as he tended a pan of thin gruel. 'What you know I don't know?'

Billy gave him a sour look.

'Who says I'm perked up? I'm just trying to keep my morale up. My guts is shouting for some real food and I'm just trying to forget what a mess we're in!'

Abel looked at him suspiciously.

'You got a stash of grub we don't know about? All that twaddle about your guts doesn't wash with me! I think you know something, Billy, so out with it!'

'Mind your own goddamn business, Sambo, or your big mouth is going to get you into trouble!'

Abel drew himself up to his full height, his eyes sparkling with anger.

'Who're you calling Sambo? I'm in two minds to give you the hiding of your life, white trash!' He flexed his muscled arms, hands clenched, ready for action.

Billy surveyed the truculent chin and the bulging muscles honed to hardness by years of working in the fields and decided to back off. It was essential to be fit for the journey ahead.

'All right . . . all right! Just mind your own business and I'll not call you Sambo again! Now let's get on with the chores and forget the whole thing.'

Abel grunted. He was still smarting. He was particularly sensitive about being called Sambo. His late master used to call him that when he kicked him.

Later, he saw Hunter looking over the horses and on impulse went to him. Looking around he saw no one was about and he spoke softly to Will as they both sheltered between two horses.

'Boss, I've something to report.' He looked nervously around, wondering where Billy was right now. Will eyed him narrowly.

'Something serious, Abel?'

Abel looked uncomfortable.

'I'm not sure, boss. It's just that Billy was acting kinda funny today.'

'What kind of funny?'

'All perky-like, as if he'd had good news. It began after he packed Tommy's warbag. I asked him what he was so cheerful about and he got nasty. We nearly came to blows.' He told Will what had happened between them. 'So you see, boss, I don't really know anything but I thought as you should know about it. I hope I did right?'

Will patted his arm.

'You did quite right, Abel. Don't say anything to the others. Just forget what happened and leave things to me.' Abel nodded and left Will examining the horses' legs.

Will's mind had jumped to Tommy. Would Tommy tell Billy about the gold? He trusted Tommy and didn't want to believe that the boy he looked on as a son would betray his trust. Then he remembered Tommy's weakness. Had Billy plied Tommy with booze? Had the boy let slip about the gold? He made his mind up there and then and went quietly to the wagon, ostensibly to bring out another sack of coffee and check the dwindling stock of foodstuffs. He unearthed the chest from under some sacks and opened it. Then taking one of the empty sacks he quickly transferred the contents of the chest. Now all he had to do was fill the chest with something just as heavy. But what? Then he grinned as he reached for a bag of horseshoe nails. He weighed it. Yes, it was near enough the weight of the gold. Those horseshoe nails would be no great loss as they wouldn't be needed now they had lost so many horses.

He closed and locked the chest and left it covered by the original sacks. The gold he carried along with the sack of coffee and left the wagon. As he strode over to the cookhouse he quietly stashed his sack of gold inside a horse-trough now packed with new snow. It was quickly hidden and covered by the soft snow. He would pick it up later.

Abel and Billy looked surprised when Will tendered the coffee.

'That last brew of yours was as weak as a new-born baby,' he grumbled. 'For Christ sake, give us a decent cup of coffee from now on. If we're low on grub at least let's have decent coffee!'

'Just as you say, boss. It's just that our stock was running low. Everyone will appreciate it, boss.' Abel took the small sack and opened it, ready to brew up.

Will nodded and watched Billy who had virtually ignored him.

'What you concocting for supper, Billy?'

Billy grunted.

'Same as usual. The last of the horsemeat, some gruel for thickening, some yams and a handful of beans and some panbread. We're running short on flour. Maybe you should have a word with Broadbent and the reverend. They seem to have contributed the least. Betsy says they've no spare food left. She gave us what she had a few days ago and I think she was telling the truth.'

Will nodded.

'Yeah. I'll have one last try. If the worst comes to the worst we'll have to search all the wagons and see if anyone is holding out on us. We've got to pull together if we're to survive!'

Suddenly Billy turned and faced Will.

'You think Tommy will make it?' he said baldly.

'I reckon so,' Will answered evenly. 'He's the only man amongst us who can. Why do you ask?'

Billy shrugged.

'Just that it seems risky him setting out on his own. Maybe someone should go with him! What if he he fell down a crevice or he met up with wandering Indians!'

'I think Tommy's too experienced to fall down into a snow-covered crevice and as for Indians, Tommy could smell 'em a mile off! He'll not be caught by marauding hostiles!'

Billy went back to his job of scraping horse-meat off some bones. Will left them and was thoughtful as he went about his business. Maybe Abel had been right and Billy had something in mind. . . .

That night Will remained on watch. He made no announcement but he watched his own wagons and was rewarded by seeing a shadowy figure dodge from one wagon to another. Will grinned to himself. So, Abel had been right! Billy was reckoning to light out and take the chest with him!

He watched Billy's thorough search of his wagons with interest and nodded as the crouching figure jumped down holding the bulky chest in his arms. He'd guessed right. Billy was reckoning on using Tommy to lead him out of the wilderness. Thank God he'd locked the chest! Billy would not break it open until he was well away and clear. Will smiled again and then wondered whether he should tell Tommy what to expect, then thought twice about that. If Tommy was in on it he would tell Billy that he'd made off with a load of old horseshoe nails. He decided to leave well alone.

When dawn came Will watched Tommy leave on his own horse, taking one of Will's as a packhorse. He had given him an extra box of shells and told him to be extra vigilant. He wondered if he would ever see Tommy again. He'd hoped Tommy would have given him a hint of any trouble but there was no sign. He watched him go with great sadness.

He turned away. He had other pressing business to attend to. There was the vexed question of food being hoarded. His own stock of food was going down fast, for he was responsible for his drivers' rations. Andrew Witherspoon relied on the goodness of others, as his own wagon had been destroyed. Doc McLochry, Eddie Doolan and Zac the peddler were travelling at the expense of Will Hunter, and so it was up to the

Broadbents and the Logans to share their stocks of food. Abel had used all Lance Pritchard's foodstuffs as soon as he was freed. It was alarming how fast the food had dwindled away. Starvation was now stalking the camp.

That evening, as they huddled in the cabin around the one fire kept going in the pot-bellied stove, Will made it stark and clear.

'If anyone is hoarding any food of any kind, now is the time to bring it out and declare it!'

Everyone looked at everyone else.

Two of the drivers produced two bottles of liquor each and put them shamefacedly on to the rickety table. Doc McLochry took charge of it.

'I'll take that,' he said tersely. 'I regard it as medicine at this time. We're low on pills and potions. A slug of whiskey might come in handy if I have to dress a wound. You never know!'

Some of the men looked sceptical. They all knew the doc's weakness for booze.

Jack Broadbent spoke up.

'Look, we've got a bag of corn and some molasses we'd forgotten about and some sugar and salt . . .' His voice trailed away and he looked shamefacedly around him. 'I'm sorry. We really did overlook them.' He bit his lip as the men around him looked at him with contempt.

'All right,' Will said, looking around. 'Now if any of you have forgotten anything that should be declared, just turn it in at the cookhouse. We must know exactly how much grub we have left. What about you, Reverend? Are you holding anything back?'

Mordecai Logan looked affronted. His voice boomed as if he was in the midst of one of his hell-fire sermons.

'I assure you, Mr Hunter, sir, as God is my witness, I am not cheating! My wife is in control of whatever reserves we have. If we have anything undeclared it will be of her doing! My wife and my son take charge of the everyday problems of life and I am free to attend to my spiritual calling. We are all in the hands of God and if we repent our sins he will lead us out of the wilderness! I say unto you . . .' His voice boomed forth only to be silenced abruptly by Will Hunter who drew his gun and aimed it at the preacher's chest.

'That's enough Logan! We're not in the mood to listen to your rantings and ravings! Just tell your wife and son that if they are keeping any foodstuffs secret, they must bring them by this evening to the cookhouse or else your rations will be cut. Understand?'

They glared at each other.

'How dare you point that gun at me and speak in that tone! As God's my witness, you'll pay for this!' The Reverend Logan stomped away.

The silence amongst the gathered men spoke volumes. Eddie Doolan spat in the snow.

'What with him and this bloody snow, it makes you wonder whether there is a god,' he said dolefully. 'He sure is a bad judge of character, that is if there is a god up there looking down on us. I wonder what he's thinking now!'

Some of the men laughed. Others looked worried. Doc McLochry spoke up for the majority.

'Whether there is or there isn't, the real question is, can we hold out until Tommy gets to Fort Churchill and how long will it be before the troops hack their way through . . . if Tommy makes it!' He looked around at all the men. 'Will's right. We've got to pull together and no cheating. We've got to be one big family and be there for each other.'

Betsy, who'd drawn close to the men now said spiritedly:

'We're all responsible people. We've all to pull our weight. Maybe it's time for all of us to have certain chores to do and not leave all the worry and botheration for Will here.' She turned to Will with a smile. 'I'm willing to take my turn at the camp chores and I know my girls will too. Anything you want me and them to do, Will, we'll do with pleasure!'

Will tightened his lips as he heard a snigger behind him. It was the wrong time for lewd thoughts and he knew that Betsy's offer and support were genuine.

'Thank you, Betsy. Perhaps you and the girls could help with the cooking. I suspect one of our cooks has gone missing!' There was a general murmur and stir at this and everyone looked round for Abel and Billy. Abel was to be seen but now it was plain that Billy was missing.

Mick Mayo swore.

'Has the bastard gone off with the scout?' He looked hard at Will. 'Did you order him to go or has he lit out on his own? Tommy didn't need a nursemaid!'

Will looked grim.

'He took off on his own and that's all I'm saying.' He turned away from the group, his back stiff and uncompromising and everyone knew that it would be no good pursuing the matter. But Billy was the main topic of conversation as they divided up the camp chores between them.

More of the old shack was chopped down into logs. It was becoming increasingly hard, for the men were now hungry all the time and fighting the cold was sapping their strength.

The next few days passed slowly. A grey mist settled down over the land. The wintry sun rarely shone down on the snow. It was now an eerie, small world.

The men took turns to dig down into the deep soft snow to find grass for the horses to augment the pitifully small ration of corn each animal got each day. They were now skin and bone and Will thought ruefully that now there was no meat on them they were no good as food and certainly in no condition to pull wagons.

The situation was getting worse all the time.

Then Betsy announced one morning that Jenny had died in her sleep. Doc McLochry's conclusion was that hypothermia, lack of food and her thin frame were to blame; privately he thought that the remaining girl would go the same way if help didn't come soon. He said nothing of his fears however. No need to distress Betsy any further. She too had lost weight and was looking old and haggard. Gone were her flamboyant looks.

Two days later, one of the drivers collapsed while dragging logs. When he was found his body was already frozen.

Will wondered just how many bodies there would be waiting for burial when the troops arrived . . . if they arrived.

Life was now a nightmare.

SIX

Tommy was finding moving through the thick snow painfully slow. His eyes roved the white world for tell-tale signs of the trail now hidden by virgin snow. Not even tracks of animals were to be seen. It was as if he and the two horses were the only things moving. He had been on the trail only since dawn and it was now noon and he knew that both he and the animals needed shelter and a break. He must conserve the energy of the horses.

Then he heard a shot. It was as if a hornet had buzzed past his ear. He turned, looked back and saw the black ouline of a figure on horseback, leading a second horse. So the bastard had been serious when he said he was coming with him.

He waited for Billy to catch up with him. Billy was laughing.

'You're supposed to be the scout, but you didn't catch on that I was following on behind.'

Tommy grunted.

'I hoped you'd changed your mind,' he muttered. Billy was still carelessly holding his gun and it seemed to be trained on Tommy's heart. 'You can put that thing away. If I die, you die too, you two-timing dung beetle!'

Billy twirled the gun and slipped it back into its holster.

'Now that's not very nice, Tommy. We've got to be pards. You and I are going to share what's in that chest. Remember?' He indicated the bulky box tied on to his pack-horse. Tommy recognized one of Will's most prized horses. He would be as mad as hell when he discovered his loss. He grunted.

'So you found it. You'll not get away with it, Billy. Will Hunter will never let up. He'll follow you to hell and back!'

Billy laughed.

'What makes you think he'll ever get the chance? We're not going to Fort Churchill. Didn't you guess we'd not head for the fort or are you just a dumbhead?' His tone was amused but contemptuous. Tommy seethed inside with anger, both for himself and for Billy's cold-blooded plan to leave Will Hunter and his wagon train to starve to death. His face did not betray his feelings. He would have to play-act as he'd never done in his life before.

'Look, Billy, I don't care a peddler's damn

what you do. I'm going to Fort Churchill and you can go on to hell and take that cursed chest with you! Keep the lot. I'll take you as far as you want to go and then when the time's right and you want to strike south-west, you're on your own. I can't say fairer than that. Take it or leave it!' He waited breathlessly for Billy's reaction. It soon came.

'Nothing doing, pard! Who in hell but a fool would give up half of what this chest holds, and you're no fool! I don't aim to settle somewhere thinking I'm safe but having to look over my shoulder for the rest of my days! No sir! You're coming with me. I'm not letting you out of my sight and if it comes to shove rather than push I'll cripple you just enough so that you can't ride away and leave me! Do you hear? The first sign that you're double-crossing me and you get it!'

Tommy breathed deeply and hid his anger. He'd have to keep a sharp look-out for Billy's first mistake. Meanwhile he would act the craven half-breed, scared shitless by a bullying hardcase. He hung his head and Billy sneered.

'Not such a clever son of a bitch after all, Tommy. I wonder what Hunter would think of you now?'

Tommy didn't answer but turned away so that he didn't betray his turbulent thoughts.

'It's no good standing here arguing and freezing to death,' he muttered. 'These nags need feeding and some rest if we are going to press on until nightfall.'

Billy eyed him suspiciously.

'We are on the right track?'

'Yep.'

'How do you know?'

Tommy's look nearly betrayed him.

'I know these mountains. I was brought up in these parts and I know every goddamn skyline. I can even tell you which of those hills houses the bones of our ancestors and which are sacred places. Snow doesn't alter terrain if you know what you're looking for.'

Billy relaxed a little and his gun lowered.

'So, we eat and see to the horses and we ride on until dark. How long will it take to reach Fort Churchill . . . if we were going there, that is?'

'If the weather doesn't worsen I can do it in ten days with luck. If another storm blows up then we'll have to take shelter. Not even I could travel in a blizzard.'

'Hmm,' mused Billy. 'I really think that what with the rations both of us have got, I can make it to San Roselle.' Then he quickly covered up his slip. 'I mean we both will make San Roselle.' He smiled, showing his teeth in what Tommy thought of as the snarl of a jaguar.

He latched on to the *I can make it.* So the son of a bitch was reckoning to ditch him on the way. He had been right in the first place. The hairs on the back of Tommy's neck rose. He would have to out-think the bastard, even if it meant leaving the trail and heading out into the wilderness, risking their food running out and both of them starving to death. But he only nodded and began leading his horses to a sheltering boulder. Then he fumbled in his saddle-bags and pulled out his warbag. From the pack-horse he took the small bag of corn. His first job was to feed his two animals. They were more important than himself if he was to get out of this mountain range. Billy did likewise. They had no means of lighting a fire, so made do with bread and jerked meat and a pull from Billy's whiskey-bottle.

Later, they moved on, silent, each wary of the other. Billy rode half a horse's length behind Tommy. He was taking no chances. Tommy, conscious of the man behind him, wondered if he would have a chance that night to stab him in the back. Billy would have to sleep sometime.

But Billy anticipated the situation when night came and they were forced to camp. Before Tommy was aware of what was happening, Billy had whipped away Tommy's guns and had him hogtied with his lariat. It took just five minutes for Billy to heave the lighter man to a nearby tree and tie him down. Then, he took Tommy's groundsheet, opened it out and rolled him on to it.

'If I didn't need you alive, I wouldn't treat you

with kid gloves!' he said grimly. He threw him his blanket. Later, he brought him his tin plate filled with bread and beef and cold chilli beans.

'Eat that,' he said roughly, 'while I light us a fire and I'll brew us some coffee.'

Then he left the camp, struggling through the snow to find any dead wood not covered by snow. Tommy writhed furiously but could not release himself. Billy sure knew how to make his knots tight.

Billy came back exhausted with a small armful of wood, grumbling about his vain search. It took quite a while before he got the fire going and Tommy bit his lip. He could have told Billy a much better way to get his fire going, but why the hell help the bastard?

The next day they went on their journey but now Tommy had no guns and one leg was tied by Billy's lariat. Billy was taking no chances.

The third night Tommy sat and watched Billy get drunk. His own guts twisted as he smelled the good liquor. His tongue licked around his lips.

'Aren't you going to give me a shot?' he asked hopefully.

'No,' snarled Billy, belching and taking another snort. 'Why pour good liquor down a rotten drain? You know, it's driving me mad to know just how much gold we're carrying in that there chest! I've half a mind to open it!' Tommy had wondered too, but now, cold and more desperate as the days passed, he couldn't care less.

'If you break it open, you're going to have a job hauling it. Better leave it, Billy,' he said wearily.

'Any reason why I shouldn't open it?' Billy asked truculently. He gave Tommy a sharp look. Tommy shrugged.

'No. Please yourself. You're the boss. Me, I'm going to try for some shut-eye. It'll soon be dawn.'

He turned over to make himself comfortable, leaving Billy to mutter to himself. Suddenly he froze. Surely there had been a movement behind them? Or was he hallucinating? He risked a quick glance at Billy but now Billy was slumped, his back against a boulder and his eyes half-shut. If only he had a knife!

Then he looked quickly around again. His natural instincts were aroused. He heard an owl hoot and smiled. No owl would hoot at this time of year and at this altitude. He turned to glance at Billy. Had he registered the significance? But Billy was oblivious to outside noises. His head drooped.

Tommy waited, heart quickening. Would it be the friendly Cheyennes, or the Apaches on the prowl? And why were they there in the first place?

At last, when the tension made him want to scream, a dark shape materialized from behind a bush and several figures followed. Tommy held his breath. Sweat ran down his forehead despite the freezing cold and the droplets froze on his cheeks.

A faint snore from Billy was the only sound. Then a tall figure was standing over them with moccasined feet apart. The young chief spoke and Tommy felt a rush of relief pass through him.

'Tommy Two Feathers, it is I, Running Deer. Why has this man got you hogtied?' He booted Billy in the ribs. Billy sat up with a jerk looking wild-eyed from one to the other.

'What in hell . . . ?' He howled as Running Deer kicked his head.

'Be quiet! I am looking for the gun-runner, Mick Mayo. He was to meet me seven days ago at Buffalo's Leap. We have waited much too long and now we are looking for him. Have you seen his wagons? We have followed you for two days and are puzzled as to why you are treated as a prisoner.'

Running Deer's braves were now standing around watching curiously. They were a poor-looking bunch. They too were finding conditions an ordeal. All wore blankets about their shoulders despite wearing their traditional winter jerkins made of deerskin.

Billy looked at Tommy.

'What's the bastard saying?'

Running Deer had spoken to Tommy in the Cheyenne language. A threatening gesture from Running Deer made Billy shut his mouth sharp. Running Deer would know enough English to know what bastard meant.

'He's looking for Mayo,' Tommy answered tersely, then turned to Running Deer. 'Mayo is with Will Hunter's wagon train. They're holed up beyond the pass at the old way station. I was on my way to Fort Churchill to get help. This man was in the wagon train as a driver for Hunter. He lit out after me and he's carrying a chest of gold. Why don't you take it, Running Deer? You could buy all the guns in the world with what's inside that chest!'

Running Deer looked surprised and then laughed.

'Tommy Two Feathers, I owe you! Let's see what's in the chest.' He waved his arm to one of his men and soon the chest was hauled over to them. Meanwhile, with a stroke of his knife, Running Deer had cut Tommy free of his rope. Tommy stood up and stretched his frozen limbs.

Then they all watched as one of the braves used his tomahawk to break open the chest.

The box creaked open as all heads craned to see the gold. There were gasps of dismay. Tommy's eyes bulged, he couldn't believe what he saw! A heap of rusty horseshoe nails filled the chest! Wily old Hunter had forseen what was to happen! He'd cottoned on quick, Tommy thought with admiration. The old soldier was on the ball! He smiled when he heard Billy's howl of rage, quickly stifled by another kick, this time in the face from Running Deer.

The young chief turned to Tommy.

'Is this some kind of trick?'

Tommy shook his head.

'I'm as amazed as you are.' He glanced at Billy and then said softly: 'I think Will Hunter saw into the heart of Billy, known as the Goat! His heart stinks just as his body does!' The Indian nodded.

'What shall we do with him? It is your decision.'

Tommy considered. A quick death would be too easy.

'Let him live. Hogtie him to a tree like he did me. Then it is up to the gods as to his fate!'

'Very well. It will be done.' Running Deer motioned to two of his braves who sprang forward, hauled Billy to his feet and hustled him away to a nearby tree where he was strung up like a side of beef. He screamed.

'You can't leave me here, Tommy Two Feathers! You're my pard, remember?'

Tommy looked at him and spat in the snow.

'I was no pard when you roped me up like a

steer, Billy. You're lucky to be alive! Now it's up to the gods!'

'Don't give me that shit! Come on, Tommy, tell that arrogant bastard to let me go! I'll make it up to you both, I swear it!'

Running Deer bounded over to him and punched his mouth. Billy spat out blood and teeth.

'If it wasn't for Tommy Two Feathers, I'd string you up over a slow fire,' Running Deer said in good English. 'Twice you have called me a bastard and my patience is wearing thin. Be lucky you have no blisters on your arse!' He turned to Tommy. 'You owe me, Tommy Two Feathers. I shall take this man's horses and what they carry. We are starving in this wilderness. We will now go and find Will Hunter's wagon train. We want the guns from Mayo. The Apaches are on the warpath again and aim to surprise us during the winter season. We need those guns badly.'

Tommy nodded.

'I shall go on to the fort. Tell Hunter his ruse paid off and Billy is paying the price.'He grinned. 'Tell him to expect me and the troops in less than three weeks.'

The Indian nodded and laid a hand on Tommy's shoulder.

'May the gods go with you!'

Tommy put a hand to his breast. 'And with

you too. We shall meet again.'

He watched the small group disappear into the mist taking Billy's horses with them, then went to inspect his own horses. Both whinnied at his approach. They were as eager as he was to get away from this place. He saddled up, mounted, then walked his packhorse a few yards until he was close to Billy, who was now sagging in his bonds. Billy raised his head with difficulty. His eyes looked wild. Tommy turned away from their accusing stare.

'You murdering half-breed bastard,' Billy mouthed. 'I hope your mother rots in hell!' Tommy's face hardened. He never liked any comment about his parentage and especially about his mother. He was tempted to shoot Billy and his hand went to his gun. He saw Billy's eyes watch the movement. The son of a bitch was goading him into shooting him! He smiled and thrust the gun deeper into its holster.

'It's no good, Billy. You can rant and rave as much as you like. I'll not shoot you! I want you to die inch by inch, not because you strung me up but because you betrayed a man who'd given you a second chance! Will Hunter knew you were on the run and he trusted you. You broke that trust. You're nothing but white trash, Billy. I hope you live quite a while, buddy. You deserve it!' With that he kicked his horse. 'Walk on,' he said, and the two horses ploughed their way through the deep snow.

Will Hunter looked down at the man who was supposed to be on guard. There was no life in him. He lay, a stiffened corpse, his gaunt face reflecting the last few days of near-starvation. Will himself was only keeping going by strength of will. All he wanted to do was slump down somewhere and sleep and he knew that was what he should not do. That was what had happened to this poor fellow. He'd been overcome with sleep and had frozen to death.

He was now the fourth man to have died of starvation and cold. Food was running out fast. They had even taken to scraping the lean meat off a horse and put it in the stewpot with a thin gruel. Their coffee was all finished and it was becoming increasingly hard for the fittest of men to gather more wood from the dwindling pile of logs that had been the old shack. Soon, they would have to forage again for more wood and Will knew that none of the men still strong enough to move around would be capable of fighting the snow and moving in ever increasing circles to look for frozen dead wood.

A few more days would be too late.

Abel and Betsy, both now gaunt and much thinner looked up at him as he approached.

'How much food have we left?' he asked abruptly.

'If we keep to the present rations we can hold out for a week,' Betsy said despairingly. 'If those whom Doc are treating die, we can last another couple of days. I hate to say this, Will, but putting gruel down a dying man's throat seems a waste!' She sighed. 'I never ever thought I should say a thing like that!'

'You think we should just let them die?'

Betsy's face screwed up as she tried to restrain her tears.

'Oh, Will, I don't know what to think! It makes sense, but . . .' her voice trailed away. She hung her head and Will took her in his arms. She rested her tired aching head against his shoulder.

'Betsy, don't feel guilty about this. You've done your utter best in this bad situation. You've proved yourself, Betsy, the way you've coped. You're helping with dishing out the rations and when Doc wants you, you're there for him. He couldn't manage all the sick if he didn't have you to help him.'

'I try my best,' she said with a sigh, 'but as the days go by, I lose hope. I think we're all going to die, Will!'

He shook her sharply.

'Don't think that way or you'll just give up as some of the others have done! You've got to fight that feeling, Betsy!'

'The reverend says it's a punishment on us all for our past sins. I'm a sinner, Will. I should have married a man my folks wanted me to marry, but he was as old as my pa and I ran away. The only way I could survive was to become . . .' She stopped short at the word whore, but Will understood and held her close.

'Stop belittling yourself, Betsy. Believe me, you and girls like you, did us men a favour. You'll never know just much you mean to lonely men who live most of their lives in a man's world! So stop it, Betsy. Forget what that goddamn preacher goes on about! He forgets he's a sinner himself! Everyone is at some time in their lives!'

Betsy sniffed and wiped her nose on her sleeve.

'I'm sorry I kind of broke down. I'll not do it again.' She sighed. 'I'd better go and find Abel and check on what we've got left and if we can make some kind of a stew. God knows what it will be!'

She turned away from him to leave but Will stopped her by holding on to her wrist. She looked up at him, surprised.

'If we get out of this mess, Betsy, I want the chance to meet up with you again.' He went on hurriedly as he saw her eyes open wide. 'I don't mean just the usual thing.'

'What do you mean, Will?' It was said softly.

'I mean I want to marry you,' Will blurted out in a hurry, all thoughts of his widow-woman forgotten. 'Would you consider marriage, Betsy? I know it's the wrong time and everything but it will give you something to think about in the meantime.'

She gave him a happy smile and he got the impression of what she would be like in better conditions.

'Oh, Will, I don't need consider it. You've given me a reason to go on living! Of course I'll marry you! No man has ever asked me before!'

'Come here then and let's seal it with a kiss!'

Will was smiling as he watched her hurry away. The kiss on the lips had awakened a renewed energy in him. By God, he would see that they had a future together!

He went to help the men scrape snow from the grass around the camp for the horses. They were moving further afield in a desperate attempt to keep the horses alive. The corn was finished and each morning a skin-and-bone nag would be found dead in the corral. The men were weak and worked slowly, often slumping to the ground as they tried to break up the frozen snow.

Abel would accompany them and if an animal had a little meat on its bones, Abel would cut and slash before the corpse got too stiff to handle. It was the thin horsemeat gravy that was keeping them all alive, with a little millet and anything else that could be used. There was no salt now and they were on the last sack of hard-tack biscuits, which could be soaked in the thin watery soup. They had survived on two such meals a day. Now they were down to one meal a day eaten at noon.

Will now reckoned they had just enough horses left to pull one wagon for each family. If help did not come soon most of the wagons would have to be left behind.

He looked anxiously at the sky. Would Tommy make it? More important, would the troops arrive in time or would they get here after everyone was dead? The thought chilled him, then he thought of Betsy and her pledge to marry him when they were eventually saved. He swore. Goddamit! There must be something they could do rather than sit here and wait for death or delivery!

He called a meeting of his own men. He looked them all over. All of them were only half the men they had once been and Doc McLochry had shrivelled into an old man.

'I've called you together, men, because I want to know your thoughts about trying to leave this place. I reckon if we could make a start, then in perhaps a week we might meet up with the troops from the fort and we'd have food in our bellies that much sooner. Is it worth the risk?' He looked around at them all to see their reaction to the plan.

Mick Mayo scratched at the lice in his beard. It made a harsh scraping noise that irritated Will. It made his own beard itch.

'I dunno, Will. We'd have to dig our way out every foot of the way and there's no telling when another blizzard will come up. We wouldn't even have Tommy to keep us on the right track! I think it would be madness, boss. At least we've got shelter here and that pot-bellied stove. On the trail we wouldn't even be able to have a mug of boiling water to unfreeze us! I think you're mad to think of it, Will!'

The others agreed, nodding heads.

'You try scraping snow for them there horses every day, Will,' Zac said shortly, 'and you'd know that we couldn't dig out the trail every day. No sir! We all feel like babes again, with no strength. I've no muscles any more!'

'So you're willing to stay here and watch everyone die?'

'Goddammit, Will! Those troops will get here!'

'If Tommy makes it! What if he doesn't and he's laid out somewhere, a stiffened corpse?'

Zac grunted.

'If anyone could make it, Tommy would! He knows this country like the back of his hand!'

'What if he came up with a wandering band of

Apaches? They would kill him for the grub alone, never mind him being part Cheyenne!'

Zac shrugged again.

'Tommy wouldn't let a band of Apaches catch him. He's too smart for that. I say that Tommy will get through and we can look for the troops coming any day now!' The others agreed, so Will put his plan out of his mind.

During the next two days the wind rose and snow showers blanketed the ground again. Then one morning as Will wearily split planks for the stove, he stopped in surprise when he looked up at the far skyline and saw a bunch of dark figures silhouetted against the sky.

He hollered a warning to those who were clearing the newly drifted snow from around the camp. The men looked up lethargically from their shovelling, their reflexes slow. They stared at the small black dots getting bigger as they made their way down from the high ground.

Mick Mayo came to stand beside Will.

'Who do you think they are, Will?'

Will screwed up his eyes the better to see against the glare of the new snow.

'Can't tell yet. Could be Cheyennes and yet could be Apaches out hunting and got out of their territory. We'd better get the guns out, Mick just for fear they're up to no good.'

Mick hastened away and Will shouted to the other men:

'Get your guns, boys. We might be in trouble!'

There was a scramble to pick up their guns and be ready.

The Reverend Mordecai came to see what the fuss was about. Will ordered him to take cover and tell Broadbent and the womenfolk to keep their heads down. The Reverend snorted. He would warn the Broadbents but he'd be damned if he would go near Betsy and the depraved girl with her. Will's punch on the jaw knocked the preacher to the ground. He glared up at Will, as Will bent over him, breathing heavily.

'You warn Betsy, for if I hear that you disobeyed me, you'll get no more food from us, do you hear? No more! You will have to fend for yourself in future and you can pray your heart out that your god looks kindly on you, you hypocritical bastard!'

The preacher crawled away and Will turned back to watch the newcomers. Now he could see that they were Indians and not a bunch of bedraggled cowboys. Then Mick Mayo was by his side, handing him his long-range Spencer rifle. Mick took a look and burst out laughing. Will looked at him stupidly. Had the man gone crazy?

'What in hell . . .' he began, then Mick pointed to the Indian riding a little in front of the others.

'By God, that's Running Deer! I know the way he sits his horse. Head thrown back. He thinks he's the reincarnation of the Great Spirit himself! At least that's the impression he gives his followers, and he's come looking for me! I was supposed to meet him more than a week ago. Remember? You didn't approve of my being an Indian-lover! Now it pays off!'

Mick Mayo walked out to meet the small group. Will and the other men watched the greeting and the conversation that followed, all now relaxing and waiting.

Mick walked by the side of the Indian chief's horse. He looked grave. Will reckoned Mick had bad news from Running Deer.

Eventually the party stopped a few yards from Will. He went forward to greet Running Deer in the fitting manner which the chief would expect. He raised his hand and said 'How!'

Running Deer nodded and then looked at Mick.

'My friend here speaks well of you, Will Hunter. I have told him of our meeting with the half-breed, Tommy Two Feathers. We saved him from certain death and if the Great Spirit wills it, he should have reached Fort Churchill by now.'

Will pricked up his ears.

'You saved him from death?'

The chief nodded gravely.

'He was highjacked by one of your own, Will Hunter. He was bound and led like a dog when we came upon him. The man called Billy the

Goat – and he smelled like one – was using him to track their way to the fort. No doubt Billy would have killed him when he was of no more use.'

'What happened to Billy?'

Running Deer smiled.

'Tommy Two Feathers didn't want him killed, even though he was wounded. We did what Tommy wanted.'

'And what was that?'

'We hung him from a tree and left him to freeze to death!'

Will nodded. He could understand Tommy not wanting a short sharp bullet ending Billy's life. There was a lot of Indian in Tommy. Then he remembered the chest that had gone missing.

'Did you by any chance see a chest?' He was startled when Running Deer laughed.

'Yes. I was there when it was opened. I understand Billy thought it contained gold but someone with a white man's sense of humour had filled it with horseshoe nails. Are you that humorous man, Will Hunter?'

Will nodded and they laughed together.

Then the Indian made a gesture to one of his braves who came forward leading a pack-horse.

'I am here to trade guns, Mick Mayo. I have here the American dollars we agreed on and I can also let you have half of Billy the Goat's grub. You look as if you could use it.'

The men listening behind Will and Dick perked up. All hoped for coffee. It had been a long while since they warmed their bellies with coffee.

Mick nodded.

'You can take the wagon. There's dynamite too, so go carefully, but you'll have to use your own horses to pull the wagon. We can't spare our horses.'

So the deal was done. Soon, the pack-horse was unloaded and the grub Billy had filched from the meagre stores was halved and carried hurriedly to the shack and to Abel and an amazed Betsy. She knew it was a sign from God.

SEVEN

The euphoria of getting extra food was soon over. Betsy realized that even if they rationed the meagre supply to the minimum, it would only cover the next two days. She was in despair, but, remembering Will's lecture on thinking positively, she hid her feelings from Abel and the rest of the men.

But Will had taken the situation in at a glance. He knew the value of the supplies was as a morale-booster. It put heart and hope into men who had grown weary both mentally and bodily. His hope now lay in Running Deer.

They were sitting outside around a camp-fire which the Indians had built. Will had watched interestedly as they dug a deep hole in the snow until they came to the frozen earth, then cleared a patch big enough to sit around a small fire. The fire had been alight now for several hours and Will couldn't believe how the heat filled the deep hole which also sheltered them from the wind. The Indians certainly knew how to survive these wintry conditions.

He looked curiously at Running Deer, who was smoking a long carved wooden pipe. He'd offered it to Will earlier; he had taken a few puffs to be polite.

'Now that you've got your guns and the wagon, how do you propose to get it back to your village?'

Running Deer looked surprised.

'No problem. We dig our way through and when possible we cut down a tree after praying to the god of the earth for a blessing. Then we harness it to two of our horses and we drag it over the snow – something like a white man's plough. One rope will be shorter than the other, so the snow is pushed to one side and so we can ride the trail.' He smiled. 'So easy. No problem!'

Will sat back with shock. Why hadn't he known of something like this? But of course he'd never travelled in these conditions before.

'Could we come with you? Ride behind you? Our men would help with the digging . . .' his voice trailed away. He couldn't vouch for the strength of the men with him.

Running Deer nodded as if he understood.

'You may travel with us.' He shook his head. 'I do not expect your men to be much help but that would be no loss. If we want to move this wagon we must do the work whether you come with us or not. Perhaps your men would be useful in other ways.'

'Oh? How could we help you?'

'We are a small group and we know there are Apaches roaming in these parts. They will be desperate for food and ammunition because they are so far from home. We may be attacked on the way. Your men would help us to keep them at bay!' He showed his teeth in a fierce grimace. 'I would welcome a skirmish with those murdering devils! The Apaches killed my brother and my father and so I have no time for them. I think it is the will of the Great Spirit that you had to wait here so that you can help us!'

Will looked at the chief in astonishment. Surely he didn't really believe their ordeal was foreordained so that they could help a bunch of Cheyennes? But Running Deer had the look of a seer, so Will kept his mouth shut. But he had other things to think about.

'When do you reckon to move out?'

'Tomorrow at dawn.'

'Then I must leave you and go and warn the rest of the men to be ready to follow you just after dawn.' He gave a wry smile. 'It will be a hard job persuading them to be ready. They've lost heart!'

Running Deer frowned and sat up straight, his chin thrust out aggresively.

'You are their chief! There should be no persuading! You order them to be ready. Be a real leader! Threaten them! Tell them that those who do not obey will no longer ride in your wagon train! You and those with you, will be ready to ride at dawn. The fainthearts will be left behind!'

Will nodded his head. Never before had anyone spoken to him, an experienced wagon master, in that tone before. He looked at Running Deer with respect. It had taken an Indian to spell out what should have been clear in the beginning. He was the boss and those travelling with him should have known that from the start of the trip.

'Thank you for reminding me of what I should be. I have grown somewhat careless during the last few years. I have never led a wagon train in these conditions before. I should have realized that I should take firmer control. Thank you.'

Running Deer smiled and gave a little nod.

'Not to worry, my friend. I learned the hard way how to control my young braves. Believe me, there are some hotheads amongst them!' He grinned. 'We all have to learn as new problems arise. I need your help just as much as you need mine!'

Will was thoughtful as he left Running Deer and his close aides to smoke their peace-pipe and pray to their Great Spirit for success on the morrow.

Eddie Doolan and Zac listened quietly when Will announced that they were leaving early in the morning but some of the others, Andie Witherspoon amongst them, demurred. They wanted to wait for the military to rescue them. They were worn out and the thought of the trek through the snow was appalling.

'Right!' he bawled. 'All those who want to stay behind can do so at their own risk! I've given the order to be ready to ride and by God, I'm riding out with the Cheyennes and I'm making sacrifices. I am leaving some of my wagons behind, as you all must do. Take with you just what is necessary. Remember, the less weight your horses pull, the better for them! We have the advantage of meeting up with the troopers and so saving them the hard trek to the way station. The sooner we meet up with them the sooner we have full bellies!' He stalked away, heedless of protests and accusations.

Walking with renewed energy he made his way to Abel and Betsy. Abel was alone. He reckoned Betsy was with young Annie, trying to coax her to eat some thin gruel. Abel shook his head.

'I think the girl is dying but Betsy won't have it. The kid's vomiting every time Betsy tries to feed her.'

'Hell, I'm sorry.' Will passed a hand across his forehead. Annie had been such a cheerful kid during the first weeks of the trek. He sighed.

'I'm just here to tell you to be ready and packed up. We're moving out at dawn.'

Abel's eyes opened wide.

'We're going to gamble on it?'

'It's our only chance, to travel behind Running Deer and his wagon. He's got this strange idea of dragging a tree trunk in front of the wagon and shifting the snow from the trail. It might work and we can follow behind.'

'You don't think they'll jump us later on?'

'What? Running Deer? Nope! He and Mayo are old friends and the chief needs Mayo from time to time. I think we have a good chance of making Fort Churchill if we tag along with them.'

Abel shook his head.

'I never thought we'd trust an Indian!'

Will gave him a hard glance.

'We've got to learn to trust folk, Abel. I trust you, no matter what you are supposed to have done. So, get moving, mister and be ready to ride in the morning.'

He went on to Betsy's wagon. She was standing beside it talking to the preacher's son. The boy's white haggard face showed he'd been crying.

'What's happened?' Will asked sharply and Betsy turned to him with a worried look on her face.

'Mattie here says his father's gone crazy. He's not been allowed in their wagon for days. He's had to sleep under the wagon, now that they've only the one. He hasn't seen his mother for days. He comes and gets their rations and his father takes his and his mother's into the wagon and he has to eat outside. He's frightened for his mother. He says that last night his father was calling on God all night and he was ranting on about the Lord taketh and the Lord giveth, and then Mattie heard him laughing like a maniac. Have you seen the reverend lately, Will?'

'Come to think of it, the last time I saw him was when he was crawling away when I punched him. Jesus! I hope I'm not to blame for sending him crazy! I only punched his jaw!'

'I think we'd better go and see him.'

'What about Annie? How is she?'

'She's sleeping. I managed to get a few spoonfuls of gruel into her and she kept it down. I'll come with you—'

'No!' He cut her off sharply. 'You stay here with the boy. If there's to be a confrontation, perhaps the boy shouldn't be there.' His eyes locked on Betsy's and she understood.

'Yes, perhaps you're right. He would only take it out of Mattie if he thought the boy had been talking. Come on, Mattie, you help me with the stove in the cabin. Abel will want fresh firewood for the morning.'

Will turned to her.

'I forgot. We're moving out in the morning.

We're following on behind Running Deer. Abel knows and he's already packing up.'

'But Will . . .'

Will shook his head at her.

'Not now, Betsy. Just look after the boy and then get ready to ride. Maybe the boy could travel with you? He could sleep alongside that idiot boy of yours!' Betsy sighed.

'Yeah, he and Pete get along real well when they meet. I'll see to them both, Will.'

Will smiled.

'Good girl, Betsy.' He threw her a kiss before he made off to the Logan wagon.

He heard the muttering before he reached the wagon. He rapped on the side because the curtains were closed. He saw Mattie's bedroll lying on a groundsheet under the wagon. So the boy's tale was true.

'Logan, I want a word with you!' It was no time to give the man his rightful title. He didn't deserve it, Will opined.

The canvas curtain was pulled aside and the preacher's white head came into view.

'Get away from here,' he growled, his eyes bright and staring. 'Get away and stay away, you heathen! You sinner who dares to violate a man of God! Stay away and don't pollute the air I breathe!' He shook his fist at Will.

'Don't give me that shit, man! I want to know what's going on. Nobody has seen your wife for days. I want to have a word with her now!'

'She doesn't want to see anybody! Just leave us alone!'

'Is she ill? If so, why haven't you called in the doc?'

'She's not ill! She just wants to be alone, I tell you! Now, go away and be damned to you!'

'That's not the attitude for a man of God to take, Logan. I insist on seeing her and letting her tell me herself! It's her right!'

'Right be damned! She's my wife and she does as I tell her! Now get!' Suddenly the preacher reached inside the wagon and Will found himself facing an old buffalo gun. He held up his hands.

'Now Logan, don't do anything stupid!'

The preacher gave a high-pitched laugh.

'Now I've got you just where I want you! I've never liked you, Will Hunter, for allowing those loose women to travel with us. Tempting us, tantalizing us and the focus of bad dreams!' Now he was babbling in a sudden frenzy. Will gaped at him. It had never entered his head that the Reverend Mordecai Logan suffered from an all-consuming lust!

'So you're a sinner like the rest of us,' he taunted. Logan threw up his head and his hands. The gun went off. Will felt the blast over his head and was knocked to his knees. For him everything went quiet; all he could hear was a ringing in his ears.

Within minutes the doc and Mayo and a couple of drivers were there. Will was helped to his feet by Doc McLochry while Mick Mayo and the drivers took in the situation. The gun was wrested from the preacher who was now looking dazed. He started to babble incoherently about the Lord taking revenge and saying over and over again: the Lord taketh and the Lord giveth!

Will, still in shock, shook his head to clear it.

'He's crazy! Take no notice of him but get inside that wagon and see to his wife. I think she needs help!'

Those words sent Logan into a frenzy.

'No! Leave her alone!' He hit Mayo a glancing blow on the side of the head. Mayo, now grim, caught his arm and twisted it up his back. Preacher or not he wasn't standing for rough stuff from the man. He held him in a vice.

'Move a muscle, Preacher, and I'll break your arm!'

Logan stood panting and glaring as Doc McLochry climbed into the wagon and drew back the canvas curtain, letting in daylight.

He sniffed. He recognized the smell. He had smelled that odour many times. It was the sweet pervading stench of death.

He picked his way through various boxes to the back of the wagon where there was a makeshift bed wide enough for two people.

There he found her. She was lying in a white flannel nightdress with hands crossed in front of her as if ready for a coffin. The doc saw at a glance that she'd been dead for several days. There were also signs that Logan had been lying by her side after her death. She looked thin and gaunt, nothing like the little plump woman who had set off on the trek.

Doc McLochry climbed down slowly from the wagon, his eyes averted from the preacher. He wanted to hit out at the hypocritical bastard. A man of God? No, more like the devil himself!

'Well?' It was Will, waiting patiently. He was thinking of the boy who wanted to see his ma.

'She's dead,' McLochry said briefly. 'Been dead for days!'

'*No!*' Logan gave a great cry. Like a maniac he broke free of Mayo and began to run. Mayo was set to run after him but Will's stentorian shout stopped him.

'Let him go! He'll not get far!'

'But he'll freeze to death!' Mayo was shocked at the venom in Will's voice.

'Better for him to die that way. How could we look after a madman? It's for the best. In the meantime we'll have to bury the poor woman after I've talked to the boy.'

Mayo nodded and went off to find his shovel.

It was the hardest thing he'd had to do in his life, to face the boy and tell him gently that his mother was dead. Mattie listened, his face frozen with grief but he never asked about his father. Betsy held him close as his shoulders shook. Then he wiped his nose on his sleeve and said quietly:

'We'll have to bury her, sir. May I go to her?' His eyes were appealing.

'Yes, son. Take your time. Betsy, will you go with him?'

The burial was hasty. There was no way they could dig a deep grave, so they compromised by scooping out a shallow trench and then finishing off the grave with hacked-out rocks to make a cairn. Mattie came one last time the following morning, before the wagon train got under way. He had still not asked after his father.

Will watched Running Deer move ahead. Two of his men walked through the thick snow leading their horses. Rawhide ropes had been attached to a tree trunk and now the horses moved slowly forward urged on by the braves. Yes, the soft snow was being pushed aside and Will's heart lightened. Now they had a better chance of survival.

Billy the Goat came slowly back from deep sleep. He didn't want to rouse himself but someone was slapping his face so hard his head rocked from side to side. It was an effort to open his eyes. All he wanted to do was sleep. He tried to defend himself, then he realized that his wrists were tied firmly to a tree.

Memory came flooding back as he gazed into the savage faces surrounding him. They were laughing and jeering. The red bastards, he thought, and instinctively spat at them. At once their faces changed. They scowled at him. The man slapping him now took hold of him by the hair and jerked his head backwards and forwards. The pain in his neck was intense but the rest of him was numb.

'Talk, white man! Who did this to you?' A fierce dark face was thrust close to his.

Billy spat again. Suddenly a knife flashed and Billy was conscious of warm sticky blood pouring from a sliced off ear.

'You will talk! Did the Cheyennes do this? How long have you been here, one night . . . two?' His head was jerked again as his eyes began to close. If they would only leave him alone . . . even the cutting off of his ear hardly registered.

The leader of the band gestured to one of his men.

'Bring wood. We light a fire under him and thaw him out and then he'll talk!' Billy was conscious of more laughter and vaguely wondered what the joke was about.

He must have sunk into a coma again for suddenly he was awake and choking. He could smell smoke and it was all around him. He struggled feebly but it was useless. He coughed and spluttered and now, feeling a searing heat at his feet, he looked down. Sweet Jesus! They were roasting him alive! He screamed and they came running, laughing and pointing at him.

'Now you will talk, white man. Who strung you up like a chicken?'

Billy's bitterness spilled over. If he was to die then so should the Cheyenne chief and Tommy Two Feathers, if the bastard hadn't got clean away.

'It was the Cheyennes. I was with a wagon train.'

'Where was the wagon train?'

'They were camped in the old way station back in the hills.'

'They have food, guns?'

'Yeah. Much food and guns!' Billy's head dropped on to his chest.

The Apache chief smiled and nodded to his men.

'We go after the Cheyennes and the wagon train. Maybe there will be white man's firewater and we can celebrate!'

There was a whoop of joy from his followers and they watched as their leader drove his war axe into Billy the Goat's chest. They left after smothering the fire, leaving Billy's body to hang frozen until spring when the vultures would smell his rotten flesh from afar and come and strip his bones clean.

The Indians rode away without looking back.

The Apache band fanned out, looking for sign. They had left the well-travelled trail so that they could come upon their quarry silently and without warning. They relied on short sharp shock tactics, a savage assault before the bewildered victims realized what was happening. They well knew the disadvantages of being in enemy territory and their chief was a master of hit and run raids.

Now, the chief, Black Bear was desperate. Far from their own hunting grounds and short on food, the prospect of attacking the Cheyennes and highjacking their captured wagon train was pleasing. Over-confident, he hastily held a powwow with the older members of his band. The young braves would take on the wagon train while the more seasoned fighters would annihilate the hated Cheyennes and they could return to their winter lodge with all the white man's foodstuffs. As an afterthought he mentioned the bottles of liquor that the white men would be carrying.

At the mention of liquor those braves who'd doubted Black Bear's wisdom in taking on the unknown strength of the Cheyennes, now became more enthusiastic.

Now all they had to do was locate the Cheyennes in this icy world and come upon them unseen.

The third day they were lucky. Black Bear, high on a snowy ridge, looked down at the peculiar sight of two horsemen leading their horses through the deep snow and dragging a huge log behind them. It was angled so that the snow was shoved to one side. Black Bear was full of admiration for the idea. He could see at a glance that it made easy work of driving a heavily laden wagon over the trail.

He looked at the wagon. It seemed to bulge and was packed to capacity, so that the canvas covering was tightly strapped across the loads within. Black Bear's guts rumbled when he thought of the foodstuffs. There would be salt pork, jerked beef and sugar and most likely some of those tins that contained peaches which in other times they'd broken open with an axe. There would be sacks of flour and coffee. Black Bear could nearly smell the aroma of coffee.

He made his way quickly down to his waiting men.

'The Cheyennes are coming with the wagon. Soon we shall eat.'

'What about the wagon train?'

'No sign of that. That white man must have been out of his head. I say we go in now and finish them off! They seem to be a small band.

We can send a small party to scout the trail and if there is a wagon train, the youths can count coup, while we see to the food wagon. Right?' Everyone nodded agreement.

So it was that as Running Deer beat a path towards the pass which would bring them through the last part of the mountain country, a scream that might have struck terror into less seasoned fighters rent the air.

The men guiding the horses pulling the tree-trunk took cover while Running Deer and his men surrounded the watgon. Will Hunter, who was still struggling to keep up and was now hundreds of yards in the rear and masked by snowladen bushes, heard the scream and recognized what it was.

'Goddammit! That's all we need, a fight on our hands with the bloody Apache! Come on, fellers, let's close the gap and get stuck in before they take that wagon!'

However, Running Deer was holding his own. At the first sound of the scream, his men had surrounded the wagon and Running Deer was breaking open a chest of rifles. One of his men was wielding an axe at a box of shells.

Black Bear had made a mistake. He and his braves had done the traditional riding around the group to intimidate them. Instead, Running Deer had coolly taken the time to load up. When the riders closed in, screaming and firing, the

Cheyennes were ready for them. Skilled at camouflage themselves, they hid under the wagon and in the deep snow and as the yelling Apaches galloped around them they coolly picked them off one by one.

Black Bear had expected to catch an unsuspecting band of Cheyennes celebrating the capture of food and very likely drunk on white man's liquor. Instead he'd caught a mountain cat by the tail!

The man riding hard beside him was lifted clean off his horse, arms flailing, an ever-growing mass of blood where his chest had been. Then Black Bear felt the close sting of a bullet himself as he hurtled away out of range. He watched, surprised. How had the Cheyennes produced so many weapons in such a short time?

Then he heard the *boom-boom* as a bunch of white men on horses which were only skin and bone charged up the opened-out trail. The *boom-boom* came from Mick Mayo, riding in front with Will Hunter. They had each thrown a lighted stick of dynamite into the path of those Apaches still on horseback.

It did the trick. The startled horsemen fled and the Cheyennes gave them a volley to help them on their way.

Will Hunter dismounted and Running Deer came to him. He held out his hand and Will took it. They were now more than friends. They were allies.

'They'll be back,' Running Deer said briefly. 'See, they have lost many men.' He pointed to the black mounds showing harshly against the snow. 'We must be prepared. They are desperate as hunger claws their vitals. You must keep your wagon train right behind us, Will Hunter, or else they will slaughter your men and take the women. If they find there is little food to be had they will rape and then kill the women too. They will not want to take starving prisoners along with them!'

Running Deer made sense, so Will and his men turned their exhausted mounts and rode back to the wagon train which had formed a circle. They found it besieged by a small group of yelling youths intent on counting coup.

One youth, yelling and wielding a tomahawk, was in the act of leaping off his horse on to Betsy's wagon. As Will and the others galloped up he saw Betsy fire her weapon. The youth's yell of triumph turned to a scream of death.

The men with Will, all seasoned Indian fighters, fanned out and as the young braves circled the wagons they picked them off one by one until at last only two of them got away. One of them was bleeding heavily.

But the cost of holding the reckless youths at bay had been dear. Jack Broadbent had a gashed shoulder-muscle which bled copiously and Doc, who'd stayed with the wagon train, was more than busy. Jack's older boy had died during the first sortie. He had been out in the open when the Apache braves struck their first blow. The boy had been foraging for wood for a fire. He'd stood no chance. The wrangler, Juan, was dead and lay with a tomahawk still buried in his chest. Pete, Betsy's young driver, had a scalp wound which Betsy tended, but she didn't reckon he would survive.

There were several dead horses and Will despaired. Now there weren't enough horses to pull the wagons. The travellers would have to compromise and leave their wagons behind. The men travelling alone would have to bunk up with each other or travel with the Broadbents or Betsy. He himself would have to leave nearly all his own wagons behind and just find space in one overladen wagon for the drivers who'd survived. There were fewer than half of the total number left. God help us all, Will muttered to himself.

He was lucky. He'd not been wounded but he was as weak as a babe in arms because of lack of food and the intense cold. He felt the life being drained out of him, day by day. How much longer could he and the others keep alive?

He was at his lowest ebb. He'd reached rock-bottom. Now all hope was gone. He couldn't face his men. He was so tired. He wanted to climb into his wagon and cover himself up with a blanket and sleep for ever.

Something in his brain stirred violently. He blinked and shook his head to dispel the depression overtaking him. He had to fight this feeling. He'd heard of men who'd given up and let themselves die. He despised such men. Called them yellow-bellied cowards and now he was fast becoming one of them!

'Goddamm them to hell!'he shouted, turning to face the merciless landscape, his fist raised in frustrated anger. Those about him looked at him in stupefied astonishment. Was Will Hunter going mad?

Doc, wearily tying a bandage around Abel's arm, said softly:

'Take it easy, Will. We fought them off! We'll make it, Will! We've got to!'

'With everything against us?' Will snarled. 'What hope have we got? Starving to death, Horses about finished. No hope of moving those there wagons! You must be out of your mind, Doc!'

'Have you forgotten Tommy?'

'Jesus! Tommy's the best scout I know but he's not a Goliath! Anything could have happened to him after he left Running Deer. I don't think he's made it to Fort Churchill, Doc. I think it was too much to expect!'

Doc did not answer but went on bandaging a thin and haggard Abel. It seemed to Will that starvation and cold affected the toughest and hardest bodies more severely than the thin wiry men. It seemed that the wiry men could conserve their energy better. Or was this his imagination playing tricks on him? As now, for instance, he was sure he could hear a bugle in the far distance. It seemed to be playing a rallying call. It reminded him of his days in the army. A rallying call! What nonsense! His brain must be disturbed!

But Doc McLochry was acting strangely. Through blurred vision, Will could see him leaping about, shrieking and shouting. Men were coming running from the wagons and Betsy too was acting wildly.

Then it came home to him that the bugle he'd heard was really a bugle and not a fantasy. Shock and elation hit him at the same time. He began to cry and the tears froze like droplets in his beard.

Doc, beaming, came and threw his arms about Will.

'What did I tell you? I knew we'd be saved! I really believed in Tommy! He's a hero and deserves a medal!'

Many hours later, they watched as a troop of mounted soldiers joined them. Tommy was riding with the captain. He grinned and waved as they came in sight.

There was not only a troop: there were two wagons and a bunch of horses being herded behind the column.

The captain saluted as they came to stop near Will who now was waiting for them, while Tommy gave a sloppy wave.

'Mr Hunter, sir?'

'Yes, I'm Will Hunter.'

'In charge of the wagon train I understand?'

'Yes, what's left of it.'

'I have with me food and horses for you. The scout here negotiated a deal with my colonel on your behalf. I have orders to help you in any way you wish. Perhaps we should camp here for two days and let my men and horses rest awhile. The going was tough. We had to dig our way here until a mile or so back there, where we found the trail cleared of snow. Most unusual but fortunate!'

Will smiled.

'That was because of Running Deer.'

'You mean Running Deer of the Cheyenne? That rebel?'

'Yes. He saved our lives. Was there no sign of him?'

'No, the trail was empty but we did find an old man frozen to death.'

'A white man with grey hair?'

'Yes. Most unsuitably dressed for this weather.

No hat or gloves. He looked as if he'd slumped down and gone to sleep. I wonder why he was alone?'

The captain looked at Will for an explanation.

Will shrugged. 'Some poor devil who got lost, no doubt.' He reckoned it was time to change the subject. 'Was there no sign of Indians or a wagon?'

'A wagon? Why would Indians have a wagon? There certainly was no sign of either, but of course there had been a snowstorm so any sign would be obliterated. Why did he clear the snow away on the trail and how did he do it?'

'He cleared a path with a tree-trunk. He used it like a snow plough. It was for our benefit,' Will hastened to add. He didn't think it necessary to tell the captain that Running Deer had bought a wagonload of guns and ammunition from Mick Mayo. No need to get Mick into trouble with the authorities!

'Right. Then I propose my men set up camp. It doesn't seem as if there's danger from the Cheyennes.'

'We did have a run in with a marauding band of Apaches.'

'What in hell are they doing in these parts?'

'Looking for food is my guess. But I figure that your coming would scare them off. I think we'll be quite safe now and we can get on the trail as soon as your men are ready to ride.'

'What about your men?'

Will grinned. 'They've survived this far with little food but they're tough. We'll be ready to ride when you are!'

The captain looked at him with admiration.

'The scout here said you could survive anything, Mr Hunter. He says you are the toughest man he's ever known.'

Will smiled at both of them.

'Thank you, sir.' Inwardly he thought of the near breaking-point when he'd almost given in and it had been Doc who'd unknowingly jerked him back to reality.

Later, he embraced Tommy.

'You'll never know what you mean to me, Tommy lad. You're my hero.'

Tommy preened.

'Yeah, I always thought I was good at what I did. By the way, about the wagonloads of food and the horses . . .' his voice trailed away.

'Yes? That was good thinking, Tommy.'

'It was the colonel's thinking, Will. He sold me the horses and the food and he holds my IOU which you will have to pay. Oh, and there's a charge for using the troops.'

'How much, Tommy?'

Tommy hesitated.

'How much? Come on, out with it!'

'Well . . . seeing as he had us by the short and curlies, he reckons you owe him eight thousand dollars!'

'Eight thousand. . . !' Will's breath gave out and he choked. 'Jesus H. Christ! It's highway robbery! The son of a bitch's taken advantage of you, Tommy!'

'Aw, come on, Will. We were between a rock and a hard place! After all, we've got that there gold, if you still have it.'

'Yeah, it's safe enough but what with what I have to pay out in bonuses and other expenses, I'm not going to make much out of this trip! I thought I'd be rolling in dollars.'

'Come on, Will. You'll still be in pocket. You'll still be able to buy that ranch you had in mind and you can marry your widow-woman!'

Will laughed.

'I've put the widow-woman out of my mind, Tommy.'

'Oh, so you're not retiring? I knew you wouldn't. Once a wagon master, always a wagon master, I say.'

'That's not quite how it's going to be, Tommy. I'm going to marry someone else.'

'Not the busty whore!'

Will grabbed Tommy by the throat and shook him.

'I think highly of you, Tommy,' he said through gritted teeth, 'but I'll not have you calling Betsy a whore! If I hear you say that word again, as God is my witness, I'll shoot you where it hurts!' He threw Tommy from him as if he was something rotten.

Tommy coughed and spluttered and held his throat.

'All right, Will, take it easy! How was I to know? If you say Betsy's your woman that's OK by me. I want no bad blood between us. Right?'

'Right! Now let's get organized. We've a fire to raise and grub to cook and we've gotta allocate the horses. So we'd better get started.'

Will felt the anger slowly draining away from him. He had been just on this side of crazy. He had to take himself in hand and what better to help him than seeing Betsy. Muttering about looking the horses over, he left a disturbed Tommy and made his way to Betsy's wagon.

She was tending Pete, with a pale and wan Annie huddled on a makeshift packing-case covered by a blanket while Mattie looked on.

Betsy looked up and saw Will striding purposefully to the wagon. It had been some time since he'd sought her out. Now she quickly left the wagon and ran to meet him after telling Mattie to watch over Pete as Will wanted to talk to her.

Already Betsy had taken on a better colour. She was still stressed and thin but knowing that Will loved her had sustained her.

Will could see what an attractive woman she would be again. He held out his arms to her. She ran the short distance between them and flung her arms about him. He hugged her close and stroked her hair as she put her head on his shoulder.

'It's all over. We've made it,' he said brokenly. 'We'll make Sacramento and when we do . . .'

'Yes?' Now she was breathless.

'We'll get hitched and we'll buy that ranch and we'll start a new life together. Our pasts don't matter. We start fresh.'

'What about Mattie and Annie and Pete, if he lives?'

'They'll come with us, and Tommy too. We'll make a home for them all. How is Pete?'

She shook her head.

'Not good. He may not live to reach Sacramento. I'm doing what I can for him but Doc thinks it's a matter of time.'

'Poor kid. At least you made him happy when it mattered. You'll need a driver, so in future I'm driving your wagon. What d'you say?'

Her hug and kiss said it all. When he left her, he went back with a lighter heart to become the wagon master again, with all the responsibilities that went with the job.

There was much to be done.